People always stare at my chest and tell me I'm turning into a young lady. But I don't want to turn into anything, yet.

Some kids in our class do. They act as though they can't wait to be teen-agers. Some girls even wear green eye shadow to school. I think it's sickening. I never want to grow up if that's how you're supposed to act.

I'm lucky my best friend Rachel feels the same way.

Annie Morrison and her friend Rachel Weiss both wish they could stay twelve forever. Everything is perfect . . . until unexpected changes begin pulling Annie and Rachel apart just when they need each other the most.

First, Annie loses her wonderful old dog, Nora. Then Rachel announces she's moving away—to New York City. Annie is sure Rachel will turn into some sophisticated city girl, leaving her behind with girls who pierce their ears and act silly around boys. But together, Annie and Rachel learn a lot about independence and loyalty—and some good things about turning thirteen.

The Trouble With Thirteen is filled with the funny, sturdy, and totally appealing people that have made Betty Miles' books so popular. All the readers who were captivated by the unforgettable character of Barbara Fisher in *The Real Me* are sure to feel the same way about Annie Morrison, who grows up in her own way in her own good time.

The
Trouble
With
Thirteen

BY BETTY MILES

A House for Everyone
What Is the World?
Having a Friend
The Cooking Book
A Day of Summer
A Day of Winter
A Day of Autumn
A Day of Spring
Mr. Turtle's Mystery
The Feast on Sullivan Street
Just Think!
Save The Earth!
The Real Me
Around and Around—Love
Just the Beginning
All It Takes Is Practice
Looking On
The Trouble With Thirteen

The Trouble With Thirteen

Betty Miles

ALFRED A. KNOPF
New York

THIS IS A BORZOI BOOK
PUBLISHED BY ALFRED A. KNOPF, INC.

Copyright © 1979 by Betty Miles
All rights reserved under International and
Pan-American Copyright Conventions.
Published in the United States by Alfred A. Knopf,
Inc., New York, and simultaneously in Canada
by Random House of Canada Limited,
Toronto. Distributed by Random House, Inc.,
New York. Manufactured in the
United States of America

10 9 8 7 6 5 4 3 2 1

Photo strip: Jennifer Fleissner (right);
Lauren Rosenthal (left).

Library of Congress Cataloging
in Publication Data
Miles, Betty. The trouble with thirteen.
Summary: Twelve-year-old Annie is unwilling
to face some major changes in her life.
[1. Friendship—Fiction. 2. Death—Fiction]
I. Title. PZ7.M594Ri [Fic] 78–31678
ISBN 0–394–83930–7
ISBN 0–394–93930–1 lib. bdg.

FOR NORMA KLEIN

The
Trouble
With
Thirteen

1

"Go get it, Nora!" I yelled. "Fetch!"

Nora started toward the stick I had thrown, yipping eagerly. Halfway there, she stopped and turned around. Then she ran back to the porch steps where we were sitting, wagging her tail frantically.

"That's the fifth time she didn't fetch it," Rachel said.

"Training a dog takes time," I said. "You have to be patient." Still, I was beginning to wonder if Nora would ever learn. If she didn't, it would spoil our whole plan.

Rachel and I had decided to sell magazine articles. I would write the articles and Rachel would take the pictures. Rachel's father had taught her to use a camera—he's a professional photographer. If you look close, you can see his name in little letters under lots of magazine photos. *Clayton Weiss*. He travels all over the world on photo assignments. That week he was in London, England.

Our best article idea so far was "You *Can* Teach an Old Dog New Tricks." I thought it up. Nora was perfect for the article because she's ten years old and she never learned tricks when she was young. My parents got her when Kenny was four and I was two, and Mom says they were much too busy teaching us stuff like not sticking our fingers in electric sockets to worry about training Nora. But she's very intelligent. She's probably the only dog in the world who knows what "Dairy Queen" means. If you even whisper those words, she runs to the car and tries to jump in. A dog that smart should be able to learn how to fetch.

Nora stood there wagging her tail.

"You're a smart dog," I said, to build up her confidence. I pointed to the stick. "It's out there—go get it!"

Nora yipped and wriggled—but she didn't take off.

Rachel stood up. "Come on, Nora. Let's go get it!" She started running.

Nora ran after her. But when they reached the stick Nora just jumped around it, wagging her tail.

"I give up." Rachel picked up the stick and started back.

"*Fetch*, Rachel!" I called, to connect the command to the act in Nora's mind.

But Nora didn't get the connection. She followed

4

Rachel back to the steps and scrambled up across our laps, panting.

I scratched her behind the ear. "You're a dumb old dog, that's what you are."

Nora wriggled appreciatively. In the sun, her fur was the exact color of honey.

Rachel stroked Nora's back. Rachel doesn't have a dog, so she shares Nora with me. Nora loves her next best to anyone in our family. Maybe she thinks Rachel's *part* of the family. Rachel and I have been best friends ever since nursery school. She's always over at my house, unless I'm at hers.

"Not to insult Nora," Rachel said, "but maybe she really is too old to learn tricks." She bent down and kissed Nora on the nose. "Why should you, you sweet thing—you know we still love you, even if you won't fetch."

Nora's tail thumped quietly.

"It's probably hopeless," I admitted. "It's just that the idea of it was so cute. But we can think of something else."

Nora seemed to understand that the training period was over. She climbed down off our laps, walked over to a corner of the yard where the sunlight came through the trees, and sank down slowly onto the grass. Right away, she went to sleep.

Rachel reached behind her for her camera bag, unzipped it, and took the camera out. She walked over to Nora, focused carefully down at her, and snapped. Nora's ear twitched at the sound, but she didn't stir. Once Nora's asleep, nothing bothers her. Rachel squatted down beside her and took another picture. Then she came back and put her camera away.

"It's so nice out," she said, leaning back against the steps and closing her eyes. "I love it when spring finally comes."

It was a warm April afternoon. The sun shone through dark clouds, turning the forsythia bush gold. Each separate little flower was lit up. There was a sweet smell of onion grass in the air. The porch steps felt warm under my jeans. All of a sudden this ordinary moment, with me and Rachel sitting on the steps and Nora curled up in the sunny yard and the spring just beginning, seemed so beautiful I could hardly bear it. It was as though time had stopped still and I was taking a picture of it in my mind to remember forever how I felt that exact, bright second. But I knew that in the moment it took to notice it, the moment would be gone: Nora would flick her ear, Rachel would sit up and scratch her ankle. And I would never have that exact same feeling again, because things are always changing.

Sometimes I wish that they wouldn't. Right then April was so perfect I wanted it to last forever. And I wished Rachel and I could stay the way we were for a long, long time before we had to change and grow up.

I'm not ready to change, even though I'm starting to

get breasts. People always stare at my chest and tell me I'm turning into a young lady. But I don't want to turn into anything, yet. Anyway, not so fast.

Some kids in our class do. Kids like Debbie Goldstein and Iris McGee. They act as though they just can't wait to be teen-agers. Debbie even wears green eye shadow to school. She and Iris go around passing notes to each other and giggling and shouting things at boys. I think it's sickening. I never want to grow up if that's how you're supposed to act.

Rachel sat up and scratched her ankle absently. "Boy. I wish it would stay like this forever."

"That's just what I was thinking!" I said. Rachel and I are always reading each other's minds like that. We probably have some kind of ESP. When we were little, we used to play we were identical twins. In some ways we are identical: we're almost exactly the same height and we both hate cottage cheese and purple is both of our favorite color. We're both twelve, except that Rachel's a month older than I am. Neither of us got our period yet, that's another identical thing. We don't really talk about it much, but I know Rachel doesn't like the idea. I know, because we're so much the same.

But we don't look too identical. I like Rachel's looks better. She has brown hair and her nose turns up at the end. She wears glasses, but they're the neat round kind. Rachel has real breasts. I just have sort of lumps. I have reddish hair and freckles and no glasses.

Rachel says she likes my looks better, but I think she just says that so we'll match.

Anyway, the same things strike us funny. Like words that bother you when you read them. Rachel's worst example is the way the *o*'s don't match in *good food*. My worst is *sweetheart*. It's a disgusting word anyway, and when you read it you read too far and get tangled in the *sweeth* before you catch yourself. Maybe other people might not think words like that are funny, but we do.

We like the same books, too. *Little Women* is our favorite. Rachel's read it thirteen times and I've read it fourteen. We've read all the *Little House* books over and over. We watch it on TV, too, but we think the books are better. For our last book report we both read *Watership Down*. It's about wild rabbits, but it's not a little kids' book. It's very mature and deep.

"You know what Debbie Goldstein was reading in study hall yesterday?" I asked Rachel. *"Now and Forever."* That's a book by John Paul Marsten about teen-age problems. I haven't read it. I wouldn't want to, after I heard Iris and some kids talking about it in the girls' room. It sounded stupid.

"I don't know why she wants to read things like that," Rachel said. "I guess she thinks it's sophisticated. Like reading *Seventeen*."

Iris has a subscription to *Seventeen*. She brings it to school and passes it around in class. She never passes it to me. I can read it in the library, if I want to.

"There ought to be a magazine called *Twelve*," I said. "For kids like us."

"If there was, I bet they'd buy our article. That is, if Nora would learn tricks so we could *do* the article."

"Right," I said, seeing the chance to use my favorite expression. "And if your grandmother had wheels, she'd be a streetcar. *And*," I went on, "we could sell an article about that to *Streetcar Life*. If there was such a magazine."

"Oh, Annie, you're nuts." Rachel laughed.

Just then Mom came to the porch door. "Rachel," she said, "your mother called. She wants you to go home right away. Your father's back; he phoned from the airport."

"Oh, wow!" Rachel said, gathering her things. "He's early. I didn't know he'd get back today." She looked pleased but a little bit worried. "Wow—I'd better hurry." She threw her jacket over her shoulder and ran down the driveway. "So long," she called back.

"So long." I watched her run down the street and go around the corner. I wondered what she was thinking. Of course she's always glad to see her father. Mr. Weiss is a big, friendly man with a fuzzy beard who hugs you like a bear and tells funny stories. He's really nice, besides being famous.

The thing is, he and Rachel's mother don't get along

that well anymore. Mr. Weiss has gone on more trips than usual this year. Each time he comes home Rachel hopes that things will get better. She doesn't say so, but I know, because that's what I hope. I'm scared of what might happen if things get worse.

2

"I just don't know where the dirt *comes* from," Rachel complained, like a woman on a TV ad. She was lying on her dining-room floor with her head in the doll house kitchen. We were giving it a spring cleaning. Rachel's father had brought her a shiny little copper teakettle from London and that got us started.

Rachel's had her doll house since we were about eight. Her father made it. It's white with green shutters, like their real house. It has ten rooms, counting the attic. When we were young we played with it in an ordinary way. We'd save our allowances and get sets of matching plastic furniture in the dime store. But now we try to make the house as perfect as we can. We have special things in every room, like the blue chest full of tiny dishes that Rachel's aunt brought her from Mexico and the fourposter bed I made her last Christmas and the hooked rug she made herself. Each room has a different color scheme. Some people might think playing with doll houses is baby-ish, but the way Rachel and I do it it's actually quite sophisticated.

"What are you getting Kate for her birthday?" I asked. Kate was going to be thirteen on Saturday. She was having a sleep-over party. It was the first time one of our friends would be thirteen.

"I don't know." Rachel pulled the kitchen table out of the doll house. "I haven't really thought about it yet."

"There isn't much time." I hadn't decided what to get either. I wasn't sure what would be good, for thirteen.

Rachel took out a kitchen chair and dusted it carefully, rung by rung. Then she started to dust another. She studied it seriously, as though it was terribly important to get the chair clean. She was bent over so I couldn't see her face. Then she set the chair down and looked at me.

"You know what?" she said, very seriously.

"What?" I suddenly knew she was going to say something awful.

"I think Mom and Dad might get divorced," she said. Abruptly, she picked up another chair and started in on it.

I didn't know what to say.

"I just have this feeling," Rachel said. "Ever since Dad came back. I can't stop thinking about it. They're acting so—I don't know—so *different*."

"Oh, Rach!" I was scared. "Did they say anything?"

"No. I think they're trying to hide it so I won't worry. But I *do* worry!" She pushed her glasses up.

"Maybe it's just in your mind," I said hopefully.

"It's not! Last night I woke up and heard them arguing in this terrible way—" She paused. "I used to love to lie in bed and listen to them laughing downstairs. They don't ever seem to laugh anymore."

I felt so sorry for her.

"I know people get divorced all the time," Rachel went on, as though she'd been working this out. "It's not that unusual. Look at Sue Nason's parents. Or Debbie Goldstein's. Look at all the worse things that could happen, like Peter James' father."

Peter is Kenny's best friend. He lives on our block. His father had a heart attack on the golf course one day last fall and just suddenly died.

"Still," Rachel said. "You don't really think that anything bad could happen to *you*. Until it does."

I know it. I often think about that. It seems as though so much that happens to you just depends on luck. Some people have awful luck. In a way I feel guilty. I always wonder how I would act if I were blind, or crippled, or if someone in my family had a terrible brain disease. If one of *my* parents died. Or if they got divorced. I can't imagine it. I wish I could think I would act courageous, like people in books, but I bet I would just be whiny.

"Oh, Rach," I said. "I'm so sorry for you!" I reached out and touched her hand.

"Yeah, thanks." Rachel smiled weakly. "Anyway, I could be wrong. They could just be having some argument, not getting divorced."

"I bet that's it," I said. I hoped that was it.

The back door slammed, and Mrs. Weiss came into the dining room. She sank into a chair. "Hi, hon. Hi, Annie."

"Hi," we both said. It was hard to act ordinary. I wondered if it was hard for Mrs. Weiss, too. She took off her sweater and hung it on the chair. She didn't look that different. Mrs. Weiss is tall and quite beautiful. She looks like a fashion model, which is what she was before she got to be a nursery school teacher. Rachel says she hated it, except that's how she met Mr. Weiss.

"Want to eat supper with us, Annie?" she asked.

She sounded very normal. I wondered if Rachel could be wrong. She does have a pretty vivid imagination.

"I can't, thanks," I said. "Kenny and I promised to cook because Mom has a deadline." Mom's a designer for a print shop. She works at home. Her work room is in the attic. When she has an important deadline, she sometimes works all night.

"I don't know how your mother does it," Mrs. Weiss said. "Working under pressure all the time."

"Mom says she doesn't know how *you* do it," I said. "She says she'd go nuts being around little kids all day."

Mrs. Weiss smiled. "I go nuts. But I love it."

"When's Dad coming home?" Rachel asked.

Mrs. Weiss stopped smiling. "I don't know. Not till late, anyway. He phoned me at work. He's having dinner with some editor who wants a picture story on Cuba."

"Cuba!" Rachel said. "He just got *home* three days ago."

"That's not the editor's problem," Mrs. Weiss said quickly. Then she smiled at Rachel almost apologetically. "Listen, how about if we go eat at McDonald's? I don't feel that excited about cooking."

"Sure," Rachel said. "Neat," she added, as though she was trying to sound appreciative.

"I better go," I said. I felt guilty at wanting to get away. I picked up my books and my jacket. "So long, Rachel," I said. "So long, Mrs. Weiss."

When I went out, the sky was pink. Everything smelled springy and fresh. I walked along trying to squelch down my worried feelings, but I couldn't get them out of my mind.

The late high school bus went past just before I reached my corner. It stopped, and Peter James got off. He saw me and waved, so of course I had to walk on up to him.

"Hi, Annie," he said. He was wearing a red and navy striped shirt and faded jeans. His hair's blond. He looked like a kid on a paperback book cover.

"Hi." I started walking along with him because he seemed to expect me to. I feel embarrassed with Peter. Not just because his father died, but also because he's in high school now. I don't want him to think I expect him to be nice to me just because he's Kenny's friend and we used to play together. I try not to meet him on the street so he won't think he has to talk to me.

"Been at Rachel's?" he asked.

"Yeah." I didn't know what to add. I hoped he wouldn't think I was being unfriendly. I took a little step to get in step with him and by mistake I bumped his arm. I hate to be so awkward.

"Tell Kenny to come over after dinner," he said when we got to my driveway.

"O.K.," I said. I could just feel him trying not to look at my chest.

"See ya, Annie." He tapped my shoulder and walked away.

I glanced down quickly to see how tight my T-shirt had looked. Just then Peter turned around. I pretended to scratch my knee so he'd think I was looking down at it.

"Tell Kenny to bring his math book," he said.

"O.K." I felt so stupid! I ran up my driveway to the back door, hoping I wasn't late.

3

"You're late," Kenny said right away. He was stirring a pan on the stove.

"I was at Rachel's. I didn't realize what time it was." I bent down to pat Nora. "Hello, sweetie," I said. Her soft fur felt very comforting. "What should I do?" I asked Kenny.

"Make a salad and set the table," he said crossly. "Get moving. The cowboy beans are ready."

"Cowboy beans" is what Mom named chili when we were little. Kenny and I used to play cowboys all the time. We played together a lot. We hardly ever do now. We used to keep our doors open and go in and out of each other's rooms. Now Kenny shuts his. Last fall when he started to go to high school he took down the sign he'd had on the door ever since first grade: *This is Kenny's own Private room. I might not be In, but just Open the Door and come in and Play with my Toys if you want*. Kenny keeps his radio tuned to WRVR, this New York jazz station. He plays it so loud that even if I knocked, he might not hear me. So I don't knock. It's funny to say this about my own brother that I live in the same house with, but I miss Kenny.

I began to set the plates around.

"What's new at Rachel's?" Kenny asked, as though there couldn't possibly be anything new. Sometimes he's so condescending.

"Her father might go to Cuba." I wanted to tell him the whole thing and have him reassure me. But I wasn't sure he would.

"I wouldn't mind being him, going all the places he goes."

"Rachel minds." I pulled the lettuce out of the refrigerator drawer. "You know what, Ken?" I couldn't stop myself. "Rachel thinks her parents might get a divorce!" I was sorry as soon as I'd said it. It was just like me to blat it out.

But Kenny acted cool. "It's probably her imagination. Rachel has a vivid imagination. Like some other people I could mention."

"Kenny, it's not! She was practically crying just now."

"Well, if they're going to do it, they're going to. People get divorced all the time. Hurry up with the salad."

How could he be so unfeeling? I sliced the cucumber carefully, holding myself in. I wasn't going to say another word. But I couldn't help worrying.

When Kenny and I were little, we used to think that if our parents argued it meant they might be going to get divorced. Once I got up the nerve to ask Mom. She didn't laugh at me. She just said that was one thing I didn't have to worry about. I always remember how sure she sounded.

"Hi, kids." Mom walked into the kitchen looking dazed. She always does when she's just stopped work. Nora jumped up on her as though Mom had been gone for days. Mom pushed her off. "Get down, Nora. I saw you an hour ago, when I came down for coffee, remember?" She rubbed the back of her neck. "I get so stiff bending over that table. This catalogue is getting me down, there's so much detail to it."

Mom had on her usual work clothes: jeans and a T-shirt and rubber flip-flops. She never wears real shoes unless it's midwinter, when the attic gets pretty cold. She says she can't think as well with shoes on.

"I'm starving," she said, pulling out a chair and sitting down. "Thanks for doing everything. How are you both?"

"O.K.," Kenny said. He'll never give you a real answer.

"O.K.," I said. I didn't want to bring up Rachel, after the way Kenny had reacted.

"How was school?" asked Mom.

"O.K.," Kenny said again.

"Fine," I said. I tried to think of something to tell her about it, but I couldn't. School seemed a long way off.

Mom said, "Well, you're not the most talkative types, either of you." She looked at the clock. "Dad should be home any minute."

I tried to imagine how I would feel if Dad didn't come home, not just one night but every night. I just *couldn't* imagine it.

My dad's unusually nice. He works in an accounting firm in New York, but he's not like a stereotype of a businessman. He has hundreds of hobbies— gardening, jogging, woodworking, climbing mountains in Vermont. He makes us special birthday cards with little cartoon pictures. My twelve-year-old card had a raccoon and a skunk with balloons coming out of their mouths, saying things like "Wow!" and "Far Out!" and "Twelve—count 'em—twelve!" My friends thought it was neat. I still have it on my bulletin board.

Nora barked, and I heard Dad on the porch. Mom went to the door.

"Come on, Annie. Get out the butter and the milk. Everything else is ready," Kenny said.

"Don't *nag* me!" I knew it was a mistake to say that when he was already mad, but I couldn't stop myself.

Kenny turned on me. "What's wrong with *you?* You're pretty touchy for someone who came home late and let me do all the work."

"All the work?" I snorted. "Opening a few cans of beans is work?"

"That's not the point. The point is, you said you'd be home at five thirty and you didn't get here till quarter to six. I don't mind fixing dinner myself—it's simpler without you, actually. But it's not fair when you promised to be on time. It's irresponsible."

Nora ran back into the kitchen and jumped up at his arm as he set the skillet on the table.

"And naturally, you forgot to feed Nora," Kenny said smugly.

"I was just *going* to!" He makes me so mad.

Dad came in. "Hi, kids. Smells good. You the cooks tonight?"

"*I* am," Kenny said. "Annie just wandered in a couple of minutes ago."

"I was just a little bit late!" I protested. "I made the salad!"

"Big deal," Kenny retorted.

Dad didn't seem to notice the argument. "How're things, Ken? Good day?"

"Yeah."

Dad smiled at me. "What's new, Coke?" Coke is his nickname for me. It's short for Coco the Bird Girl.

"Nothing much." Usually I love to tell him stuff.

Dad went upstairs to change, and Mom went up to talk with him. I got Nora's dish out and started pouring her dog chow. She jumped around, bumping into my elbow so some of the chow spilled.

"I'm *getting* it for you," I told her. "Take it easy!" I set the dish down and Nora began gulping her chow, pushing the dish across the floor toward the refrigerator where I was getting the milk. "Look out!" I said. Sometimes even Nora can be a drag.

"That dog's a real drag sometimes," Kenny said, pushing her out of the way.

"She is not! And you don't have to *kick* her!" I said quickly.

"I'm not kicking her. I'd just like to move around in here without bumping into her, for once."

Mom and Dad came in. "Oh, kids," said Mom, "cut it out, will you? Let's have a pleasant meal."

But we didn't. Why is it that when you already feel bad, everything seems to go wrong? That night Dad was upset because Kenny and I hadn't weeded the garden, and Kenny was mad because I'd used up his tape and he needed some for his history notebook. And then Mom started in on me. She got that look that means she's going to complain about something.

"I was thinking," she said, "that you and I should go shopping, Annie."

"What for?"

"Well—maybe a new skirt for spring? And that jacket of yours is pretty disreputable. What about a nice lightweight blazer instead?"

"Mom! Nobody wears those! Everybody has a jacket like mine."

"Does everybody's smell like yours?" Kenny asked, buttering a piece of bread.

I shot him my meanest look.

Mom said, "I just wish you had one that fit you better, that's all."

"I hate new jackets!" I said. "They're so stiff. This one's broken in the way I like it. Besides, it has my rainbow on it."

I spent about a week last month embroidering a rainbow onto my jacket from directions in a library book called *Embroidery Made Simple*. They should have called it *Embroidery Made Complicated*. I had to rip the whole thing out and start over about ten times. In the end, it came out terrific. Even Iris said it was neat.

"You could cut the rainbow off and sew it onto another jacket," Mom said. She sighed. "I just wish you'd consider something besides denim."

Then Dad started in. "I've seen lots of young women in the city wearing blazers. They look very smart." He smiled at me in that doting way he has. He doesn't know anything about how kids want to look.

"It would be nice if you had something new before Kate's party," Mom said, giving herself away. That was it—she was afraid I'd embarrass her in front of Kate's mother.

"Mom! It's a *sleep*-over party. We'll wear pajamas the whole time!"

"You should have some new pajamas, too," Mom

said right away. "You're bursting out of your old ones." I hate for her to talk like that in front of Dad and Kenny.

"She's growing faster every day," Dad said fondly, making it worse. "We'll have *two* teen-agers in this house before we know it."

I threw down my fork. "Why does everyone keep *picking* on me?" I drank some milk and choked on it. Kenny thumped me too hard on the back. I wiped my eyes on my napkin. My parents were looking at me as though I'd hurt *their* feelings.

The phone rang. I jumped up and ran to answer it.

"Annie!" Rachel said in a strained voice. "Are you alone?"

"No, I'm downstairs. We're eating."

"Could you go to the other phone?"

"Sure." I put the phone down. "Hang up for me, Kenny—it's Rachel."

"Can't you ask her to call back after dinner?" Dad asked.

"No I can't!" I yelled. "Some things are more important than food!"

I ran upstairs, slammed the door of my parents' room, and picked up their extension. "Hang *up,* Kenny!" I yelled into it. There was a click. Then a pause.

"Annie." Rachel's voice was so solemn I froze.

"What is it, Rach?"

"I was right. Mom just told me. They're going to."

She waited a second, then went on. "Get a divorce."
Her voice was flat. "Everything," she said, announc-
ing it like a weather forecast, "is going to change.
We're moving to the city."

4

"You *can't* move!" I told her the next day. We were sitting by ourselves in the cafeteria, with kids shouting at tables around us. A steamy hot-dog smell hung in the air. "It's exactly the wrong time," I explained carefully. "Kids need security when their parents break up. It's a psychological fact. They need their regular routine. They need their friends!"

Rachel nodded stiffly. "My parents know all that." She pulled at her hot-dog roll. "They're not stupid. They're not cruel, either. They're trying to work out the best thing for me. Don't go making things worse by blaming them. You ought to feel *sorry* for them."

"I feel sorry for *you*," I said. I was too ashamed to add, "and for me."

"Yeah," Rachel said. She started to bite into her hot dog and then she put it down. "Yeah," she said again.

"How can you move?" I pressed on. "This is your *home*. You'd hate it in the city. In some dark little apartment with no yard or anything. You'd have to go to a new school. Kids would ignore you, or else beat you up. You could get mugged on the street—"

"*Stop* it, Annie!" Rachel interrupted. "Cut it out, will you? Are you trying to make me cry in front of the whole cafeteria? I thought you'd at least be sympathetic."

"I *am* sympathetic, that's the whole point! I can't see why they should make you move."

"Because." Rachel's voice was strained. "Because, for one thing, it's better for Dad to have an apartment near his studio, instead of commuting. And he wants me to live near him. And for another thing, so Mom can get modeling work."

"I thought she hated it!"

"It pays a lot. She doesn't want to take alimony from Dad and she can't live on part-time teaching. She wants to get a day-care job and model on the side." Rachel looked at me as though she was begging me not to argue. "She wants us to be near Aunt Sylvia. And she wants me to go to private school."

"Private school! You're kidding! What's wrong with Schuyler School? People move to Madison, New York, just so their kids can go to it."

"Nothing's wrong with it; it's just that Mom thinks I should have small classes and good counseling next year. Aunt Sylvia has a friend whose kids go to Barclay. She says they love it. I'm going to the city this weekend with Mom, to meet them."

She sounded almost interested. I couldn't believe it. How could a person like Rachel even consider going to Barclay School? It's supposed to be so exclusive. I wondered if Rachel would start acting snotty if she went there. Maybe she wouldn't want me to meet her new friends. Probably she'd start wearing sappy clothes—boots with three-inch heels and quilted vests and droopy blouses like models in Bloomingdale's ads. She'd turn into a New York City teen-ager.

"So I can't come to Kate's party after all," Rachel said.

I was furious. How could she not come? I'd been looking forward to it so much. It wouldn't be half as much fun without Rachel. *Nothing* would be any fun without her. I began to really understand what her moving away would be like.

"What's the big rush?" I asked. "Can't you even wait one week to meet those stupid kids? Don't you *want* to go to Kate's?"

"Of course, what do you think?" Rachel shot back. She began to explain as though she was trying to convince *herself*. "Mom wants us to settle on a school fast, so we know what part of the city to move to. Sylvia says I have to apply practically this minute if I want to get into Barclay next fall. See, they don't accept that many kids for eighth grade. Most kids just start there in kindergarten and go right through." Her face crumpled. "They'll know each other already. They'll have their own cliques."

She looked so miserable that my anger melted away. "They'll like you, don't worry," I said.

Rachel wadded her napkin and pressed it into the mustard on her plate. "Yeah."

"Oh, Rach," I said, "I'm going to miss you so much!"

"Me, too," said Rachel.

I felt awfully sorry for us both.

"Guess what, you guys!" Kate said, setting her tray on the table and climbing over the bench, with Sue and Angela and Janie crowding over after her.

"What?" Rachel sat up straighter. I could see she didn't want them to notice anything.

"Mom's letting me get my ears pierced, for my birthday!" Kate said.

"She's having it done at Silversmiths' Saturday afternoon," Angela told us. "I might, too, if I can talk Mom into it. Want to come? Sue's asking her mom."

"I don't know, though," Sue said. "I'm sort of scared of it."

"They say it doesn't hurt at all," Kate said, unsurely.

"I'm just coming to watch," Janie said, unloading her tray. "I know Mom wouldn't let me do it. She thinks it looks cheap."

"Cheap!" Kate laughed. "It's costing me a whole ten dollars!"

"Since when did you want your ears pierced?" I asked her. I was surprised to know she'd even been thinking of it. Compared with Rachel moving it was such a little thing, but it bothered me. I wondered whether Kate turning thirteen would make all the kids start acting different. Sooner or later, they probably would. I wasn't sure if I could keep up. Everything was changing so fast! I felt miserable.

"Kate wants her ears pierced so she'll look sexy for Alan Shay!" Janie teased.

"Shut up, Janie!" Kate poked her, looking embarrassed.

Kate's had a crush on Alan Shay since we were in sixth grade. We always kid her about it. Alan's nice. He's awfully serious, though. He probably wouldn't even notice if Kate got her ears pierced. At least, I don't think he would. But the boys in our class are changing, too. Tony Albrecht invited Sue to be his date at his Bar Mitzvah, and she went. I would have been shy, but Sue said it was fun, except that Mrs. Albrecht kept introducing her as "Tony's little girl friend." She's at least two inches taller than he is.

Sue's a person who doesn't try to show off or act sophisticated. I hoped she wasn't going to get her ears pierced. I wanted her to stay the same so I'd feel more comfortable with her. Especially with Rachel gone. I glanced across the table at Rachel. It seemed disloyal to even think of her being gone, when she was sitting right there. She was twirling her paper plate with one finger. For once, I couldn't tell what she was thinking about—pierced ears, or her parents, or moving away, or what. I reached out and touched her finger, and she looked up at me and smiled. But I felt awfully lonely already.

If you're feeling bad for any reason, going to the Mall always makes you feel worse. It's so glarey and noisy. The stores are full of things you think you might like until you get up close and see how stupid they are. I went there with Mom on Friday night. She took me so I could look for a present for Kate and maybe get pajamas. "Just look at them," she said. "You don't have to buy anything you don't like."

Mom had been very sympathetic when she found out about Rachel moving. It must be hard for mothers when their kids are sad about something and they can't make it better. But Mom's quite sensitive. If you feel bad, she lets you. She doesn't keep pointing out the bright side.

She went to look at shoes, and I wandered through the Mall trying to find a present. I looked through racks of posters, but the best ones, the nature photographs, all had dumb philosophical sayings printed over them. I love Snoopy posters, but I was afraid that might be too babyish for thirteen. The smell in the candle shop got me down before I could find a good candle, and nothing in the drugstore seemed right. We've all been giving each other bubble bath for birthdays since we were about six years old. And the names are so sappy. Rachel and I always laugh at them. It's ridiculous to sit in a bathtub in Madison, New York, and wash your knees with a soap called Tropic Passion.

I was beginning to feel desperate. I wished I could just give a present without worrying about the impression it would make. I worry about stuff like that too much. Kate wouldn't care. She's not the kind of person who puts you down. But I wanted to get her something really good. Finally in the Indian store I saw a blue enamel bracelet that looked quite elegant and only cost four dollars. After I bought it I felt much better. I knew Kate would like it.

Bamberger's pajama department is called Night Life. They had racks and racks of nylon pajamas with bikini pants and smock tops. I would never wear something like that in my own house, much less where other people could see me. They were ridiculous. Way in back of them I found a rack of pretty good flannel pajamas. They were on sale, I guess because they were left over from winter. But I didn't care about that. The problem was that every single pair was marked L. They were gigantic. Shopping is so frustrating!

Everything else in the department was nightgowns. I found one rack of them that looked sort of interesting. They were made out of T-shirt material in really neat colors—purple and emerald green and a bright blue. One whole section of the rack was size **S**. The only thing was that the tops were cut very low and they had just little string ties over the shoulders. They were meant for people with real breasts. I couldn't picture how I would look in one. I wondered if I might look good. It would be funny to go to Kate's party with a nightgown like that and surprise everyone. Especially since Rachel wouldn't be there to make jokes about it. I wasn't sure which color would be the most flattering. Probably the purple. I pulled a purple gown off its hanger and held it up in front of me and went to the mirror. It felt nice the way the gown hung around my ankles. Even with my jacket and my jeans sticking out I could see it would look good.

The only problem was, I wasn't sure what Mom would say. I looked up and saw her coming into the department.

"I found something!" I called, carrying the gown up to her.

Mom looked surprised. "A nightgown! And isn't that style a little bit, well, old for you?" she asked. "Did you try it on?"

"It'll fit," I told her. "It's size **S**. It's the right length."

"I wasn't thinking about the length," Mom said carefully. "It was the front I was wondering about."

I wish she wouldn't always question my taste, as though I'm a baby or something.

"It only costs eight dollars." I showed her the price tag. All of a sudden I really wanted that nightgown. It would be neat to go to the party with something different and impress the other kids. "Isn't the color terrific?" I asked. "Don't you just love it?"

"It's nice and bright, anyway." Mom sounded as though she was trying hard to be tactful. "Have you looked at everything here?"

"Yeah. Everything else is sappy, or else too big."

Mom smiled. "Well, if you're really sure—"

"Oh, I am!"

"O.K., then," she said. "Let's go pay for it."

The woman behind the counter seemed to approve. "Isn't that a gorgeous color," she said. "And very fashionable this season." She tore off the price tag and tapped out the amount on her cash register. "You'll get a lot of wear out of this," she told Mom. "You can throw it right into the machine."

"Oh, good. But it's not for me," Mom said. "It's for my daughter."

The saleswoman looked me up and down. "Well, I don't know," she said. "On her it might not hang so good. It's cut for someone with a little bit more in the bust department." She smiled knowingly at Mom. "These kids—they just can't wait to grow up."

I grabbed the bag from her and ran out of the department. Mom hurried after me. Shoppers pushed around us in the aisle.

"Why can't people mind their own business!" I said furiously.

Mom put her arm around me. "She didn't mean

anything, Annie." She gave me a squeeze. "Look—I'm glad you found something you like. That's going to make you feel good about the party. I know you're going to have a nice time."

I really hoped that she was right.

5

When the night of the party came, I wasn't sure at all. I nearly changed my mind about the nightgown. What if everyone else brought pajamas? I thought of packing my old ones along with it, just in case, but then I decided that was ridiculous. Why *have* the nightgown if I was going to be too shy to wear it? I folded it into the Saks Fifth Avenue shopping bag I use for overnight parties, on top of my toothbrush and jacket and Kate's present, and started downstairs. As usual, just when it was time for me to go somewhere, I began to wish I didn't have to. Right that minute I would have been perfectly glad to stay home and read and watch TV, even though I knew that if I *had* to stay home I'd wish I was going to a party.

Mom and Dad and Kenny all looked up at me when I walked in. I had the feeling they were inspecting me.

"All set, Coke?" Dad asked.

"You look nice, hon," Mom said encouragingly. "You're going to have a wonderful time, I know. How many girls did Kate invite?"

"Five, I think. Except now Rachel won't be there."

"It really is a shame," Mom said. "Still, it's not as though the others aren't your good friends, too."

"Yeah."

Kenny leaned back and smiled condescendingly. "Boy, I hate to think how much noise five twelve-year-old girls are going to make. I'm glad *I* don't have to be there."

"So am I," I said quickly. "So is everyone. The very first thing we're going to do at Kate's is say a little prayer of gratitude: 'Thank goodness *Kenny's* not here!'" I love to make clever retorts like that. Kenny kept his superior smile on but he couldn't think of anything to say back. "Anyway," I went on. "It's not five *twelve*-year-old girls. That's the whole point. It's Kate's thirteenth birthday."

Kenny banged his chair down, but before he could answer, a funny noise came from the radiator. A wheezing.

"Nora!" I said. She was asleep under there, twitching restlessly. "What's the matter with her?" I asked Mom. "Why's she making that strange noise?"

"It's a kind of snore," Mom said. "I've noticed it before. Maybe she has a little cold."

"She sounds terrible!" I said. "What if something's stuck in her throat? She could choke. What if she has *pneumonia*?"

"She doesn't have peneumonia," said Dad positively. "Mom's right—she's probably got a cold. She'll sleep it off."

"But what if she keeps on wheezing like that? Maybe we should take her to the vet."

"Don't worry, Coke," Dad said. "That dog's not going to perish while you're away for one night. She's a tough old character."

My parents always take it so lightly when something's wrong with Nora. I don't know how they can be so cool. It just breaks my heart to see Nora suffer. Of course, she didn't seem to be suffering that much right then. She kept on sleeping.

"I guess she's not in too much pain," I said.

"I think not," Dad said, so quickly that I wondered if he was laughing at me. I hate for him not to be serious about important things like Nora's health.

"Don't worry, Annie," Kenny said. "I'll keep an eye on her. I'm staying home tonight—Peter's coming over."

Sometimes—just now and then—Kenny seems to understand things better than Mom or Dad. "Thanks, Ken," I said. Then I bent down to Nora. "Good-bye, honey. Sleep well. Don't do any more of that wheezing." I couldn't resist touching her lightly. She stirred and went on sleeping.

I went to the door.

"Don't stay up the whole night," Kenny said.

"Annie?" Mom said.

"What? I brushed my hair!"

"It's not that. I just thought you might like a stronger bag for your things. That one looks as though it might burst on the street."

Mom reached behind the refrigerator and pulled out a heavy brown bag with handles. It said *Shop-Rite* across the side. She doesn't understand about small details that add up to an elegant impression.

"This is fine." I shook the Saks bag by the handles to show how strong it was. It wasn't that strong, but it would hold.

"It's a very high-class bag," Dad said solemnly.

"Oh, *Dad!*" He's so crazy. I kissed him anyway, and kissed Mom and blew a kiss at Nora and waved at Kenny and went out.

Suddenly I was glad to be leaving my family and going out with friends my own age, or just about. It was a pleasant evening, cool and breezy. I stopped and pulled my jacket out of the bag and put it on. Just then I saw Peter James down the street, coming out of his yard. He didn't see me. I hurried around the corner. I wondered what Peter would think if he knew the kind of nightgown I was carrying. He'd probably be pretty surprised.

I turned onto Rachel's street. There were lights in all the houses, but hers was dark. I wondered if she was out somewhere with those kids in the city. I wished she was here instead. It would be so neat if she'd suddenly come rushing out of her door yelling, "Wait up, Annie!" Her house looked grim with the dark bushes around it. It made me think of some giant doll house that people had stopped playing with.

"Hey, Annie—wait up!" It was Sue, running across the street with her shopping bag bumping against her legs. I was glad to see her. Now I wouldn't be the first one.

"Wait till you see Kate's ears!" Sue said right away.

I had forgotten. I looked at Sue's. "Hey—you didn't get yours done. How come?"

"I don't know. I wasn't that sure I wanted to."

"Did anyone, besides Kate?"

"Not yet. Angela still might."

I was relieved. It was good not to be the only one who didn't.

Janie and Angela were standing in front of Kate's house when we got· there. "Hurry up!" they yelled, and we ran to meet them.

We all walked up Kate's steps together. Angela punched the bell and we waited in front of the door, giggling but not saying anything. You always feel a little funny before a party begins.

Then Kate opened the door.

I don't know what I expected, but she looked exactly the same except for a new red T-shirt and the little gold posts in her ears. She looked nice.

"Happy Birthday!" we yelled. Angela began giving Kate thirteen hits and we crowded around and pitched in while Kate laughed and yelled "Help!"

"One to grow on!" Sue shouted, giving a last hard whack. We broke apart. For some reason I looked across the hall into the dining room. Debbie Goldstein was standing there!

I couldn't believe it. Kate never said anything about Debbie coming. Her mother must have made Kate ask her; mothers aren't sensitive about those things the way kids are. It spoiled everything for Debbie to be there. Just the way she stood there watching us—I wondered if she thought we were acting like babies.

I was uncomfortable the whole time we had cake and presents. It made me feel unnatural to have Debbie across the table making remarks. It was O.K. when Mr. Levy and Mrs. Levy brought in the cake, and turned off the lights, and started singing "Happy Birthday to You." I love that moment when the person gets their cake. Everybody felt good then, probably even Debbie. Anyway, she clapped too when Kate blew all the candles out in one breath. And the cake was very elegant—lots of thin dark chocolate layers with raspberry jam between them and darker chocolate icing on top. But when Kate started opening her presents, Debbie had to keep butting in with some comment. Like, Janie gave Kate Tropic Passion Bubble Bath, and Debbie said, "Wait till Alan Shay gets a sniff of that!" Everyone laughed, but Kate blushed.

And Sue gave Kate a really neat pen, but all Debbie could say was how good it would be for writing secrets in the diary *she* gave Kate. And then it turned out that Angela's present was a diary too, but you could see that Debbie thought it wasn't as good as hers. Janie gave Kate a really good game, called Turn the Tables, that I would like to have myself, but I got the feeling Debbie thought games were boring. At least, when Kate unwrapped my bracelet, Debbie said it was pretty. Kate put it right on. I could tell she liked it, so that was good. And she liked what Rachel gave her—a necklace of African beads that Rachel had brought over to Kate's before she went to the city.

"Where *is* Rachel, anyway?" Debbie had to ask. "I thought she'd be here."

"In the city," I said shortly. I wasn't going to go into it. Rachel could tell people when she was ready. For a minute I felt angry at her for going off and leaving me to cover up for her. But it was really Debbie I was mad at. Why did she have to be here? What would she say when she saw my nightgown?

Kate pushed back her chair. "Let's go change!"

Everyone rushed to get their bags. I walked after them slowly and picked up mine. I stood in the hall with the bag in my hands, wishing that the party was over and that I could just go home.

6

"We can change in my room," Kate said, starting upstairs.

We crowded into Kate's bedroom. One whole wall of it is glass.

"Pull the curtains!" Debbie shouted right away. "What if somebody peeked in?"

"There's no one out there but Marvin," said Kate, pulling the drapes closed.

"Marvin who?" Debbie sounded panicked.

Everyone laughed.

"Marvin the *dog,* you idiot," Angela said.

"Oh, yeah, I forgot," Debbie said quickly. I could tell she was embarrassed. I almost felt sorry for her. But then she took this flowery makeup kit out of her bag and started rummaging around in it in a show-off-y way. "That's the trouble with giving dogs people names," she said. "You get mixed up."

"Most people can tell the difference between a dog and a person," I said quickly, angry because of Nora.

Debbie raised her eyebrows. Then she pulled out a little mirror and held it up and inspected her face very smugly. If Rachel had been there I would have poked her, and we would have cracked up.

But now I didn't feel like laughing. Everyone was starting to get undressed. They all had pajamas. Even Debbie hauled out a pair of ordinary faded blue ones. I wished terribly I'd brought my old ones along. I couldn't imagine struggling into my nightgown with all of them watching.

"C'mon, slowpoke," Janie shouted at me. "Get going!"

"I am." I pulled my nightgown out of the bag.

"Hey, that's a neat color!" Janie climbed over Kate's bed. She grabbed the nightgown and held it up by the straps. "Wow, get a load of this!"

"Hey, Annie!" Sue shouted. "Is that new?"

"Sex-*y!*" Debbie yelled.

That did it. "Your bathroom's down the hall, right?" I asked Kate. I grabbed my nightgown and ran out the door.

I locked the bathroom door. Then I got undressed. I worked my head and arms through the straps of the nightgown and pulled the whole thing down. It felt sort of tight across the top. That seemed funny, considering. I looked in the mirror. I'd put it on backward! I tugged it off again and turned it around and put it back on. This time it felt better. I checked the mirror to make sure. The nightgown drooped a little bit in the front, but the total effect was quite good.

I stared at my reflection. My eyes looked big. I think I have pretty nice eyes, actually. They're my best feature. That's what you're supposed to accentuate. I might wear eye makeup when I'm older. Not eye shadow. But just outline the natural curve of my brows.

There was a bang on the door. I jumped.

"Hurry up, Annie!" It was Sue. "We're going down."

"Just a second." I flushed the toilet so they wouldn't think I'd been looking in the mirror all that time.

They were all outside the door. Someone wiggled the door knob. "Hey, Morrison!"

"I'm coming!" I yelled. I wasn't ready to face them so I waited while they thumped downstairs. Then I came out. I held up my nightgown so I wouldn't trip and hung on to the bannister and walked down the steps very slowly. I stood in the dark at the bottom and smoothed down my skirt and pulled up my straps.

"Oh, Annie—you startled me!" Mrs. Levy came out of the kitchen.

"I was just going to the bathroom," I said, like a dope.

Mrs. Levy was staring at me. "That's quite a gown!" I didn't know how she meant it. I hoped she wasn't shocked or anything. "You surely are growing up, all of you," she said. Then she patted my arm and went upstairs.

I arranged my nightgown again and walked to the living room doorway. All the kids were lying around on the floor, laughing. But when I walked in they sat up and stared.

"Look at *her!*"

"Hey! Terrific!"

I headed for the couch, stepping over them and trying not to trip over my skirt.

"That is some nightgown!" Angela said knowingly.

I sank down on the couch and folded my arms across my chest in as natural a way as I could.

"How did you get *that* past your mom?" Debbie asked.

"She didn't care." I was sorry as soon as I said it. I didn't want Debbie to think Mom was tacky.

"*My* mom would have a fit," she said.

I wondered if Mrs. Levy might come downstairs and ask me to cover myself or something. I scrunched back on the couch and put my feet up so my knees hid my chest. I wanted to die.

Then Kate's dog Marvin started yipping, and Kate got up and let him out of the kitchen. Everyone began to make a fuss over Marvin. He jumped around yipping excitedly and wagging his tail. He didn't even notice me up there on the couch.

"Anyway," Debbie said, as though my coming in, and Marvin, had interrupted something, "the boys in our class are such *babies*."

"They'll laugh at anything," Angela said.

"Yeah," Sue said, "like, every time the word *bras* comes up in French, Todd Mitchell cracks up."

"Bra!" Janie yelled. "What's it mean?"

"It means 'arm,'" Kate told her. "It's spelled with an *s* but you pronounce it 'bra.' I don't know why the boys have to make such a thing of it."

"Because they're babies!" Debbie said.

"I guess they'll act different when they're older," Janie said.

"Don't kid yourself," Debbie said positively. "The eighth graders are worse." She leaned back against a chair and stuck her legs out in front of her. All the kids looked so comfortable in their pajamas. I felt out of it, sitting by myself on the couch. I wished Marvin would come and sit with me but I didn't want to call to him.

"You know Bob Thompson?" Angela asked. "He has this big poster of Farrah Fawcett-Majors popping out of a bikini on his locker door. And he always holds his door open so you'll see it."

"That's nothing. Danny Wilkins has a Playboy Bunny on his," said Debbie. "Lying on a fur rug with her boobs flopping."

Everyone laughed. I pretended to laugh too, but I was embarrassed. I hate that word "boobs." I wish people wouldn't say it, especially girls. It's like calling your own body stupid.

"Not all boys are like that, though," Kate put in.

"Forget it," Debbie said quickly. "They all are. Every boy in the world has sex on his mind half the time."

"How do *you* know?" Angela laughed. "Did you take a survey?"

"Yeah!" Janie shouted. "She went up to Tony Albrecht and said, 'Pardon me, I'm taking a poll, do you have sex on your mind fifty percent of the time?'"

I couldn't help laughing; it was so funny to think of Debbie asking Tony Albrecht that. "Tony'd probably say, 'No, actually, it's closer to fifty-one point seven'" I yelled out, as though I were part of the conversation.

Everyone laughed. Debbie turned around and said, "Funny!" I felt better.

"My foot's asleep!" Sue yelled, jumping up and rubbing it. Then she sat down next to me on the couch. "What I think," she said, "is that most boys would just like to be friends with girls, without worrying about the other stuff."

I think so, too, but someone like Debbie can make you wonder. "You're in for a big surprise," she said complacently. "Look at all those magazines like *Playboy*—why would there be so many if boys and men didn't buy them?"

"Not all of them do, though," Kate protested. "I

mean, like, my *dad* doesn't." She got up abruptly and went out to the kitchen. Maybe she was afraid Debbie would say her father read them secretly.

But Debbie didn't say anything. Nobody did. I guess we were all sort of uncomfortable with the idea of fathers. It's strange to think of people Dad's age being interested in naked girls.

After a pause Janie said, "Millions of men read newspapers, too."

"And other magazines. Like *Time!*" Sue said.

"*TV Guide!*" Angela shouted. "*Readers' Digest!*"

Suddenly we were all howling.

"My father reads a magazine called *Organic Gardening!*" I yelled. "It has articles about which is better, pig manure or cow manure!"

That really broke everyone up. I felt almost like a comedian.

The party got better after that. Kate brought in a tray of Cokes and popcorn, and Debbie got up and pulled a chair over. I patted the couch, and Marvin jumped up beside me. He's cute. He wagged his stumpy little tail and rubbed against my ankle. He has wiry fur, not silky like Nora's. He made me think of Nora, though. I hoped she wasn't still wheezing. But I couldn't do anything about it now. I opened a can of soda and stretched out more comfortably on the couch, with the nightgown draped over my legs. I felt sort of languid sitting there—almost like a model in a nightgown ad, except for Marvin scratching a flea on his stomach beside me.

But just when I got relaxed, Debbie had to jump up and start looking through Kate's records. "I've gotta hear this!" she said, holding one up.

As soon as Kate put it on, Debbie began wiggling her hips to the music. "Come on!" she shouted. "Everybody dance!" You could see she wasn't used to our parties. We usually just talk and eat and watch TV and stuff.

I don't really know how to dance. I never had a reason to learn. Rachel has a lot of records, but they're not the kind you dance to. I mean, who would dance to Pete Seeger singing about cleaning up the Hudson River? It would be dumb.

Angela had jumped up right away. She was dancing beside Debbie, following her movements. Then Kate pulled Janie up. "Let's try that step Marian taught us," she said. Marian's Janie's big sister. I didn't know she was teaching them to dance.

Debbie and Angela were really good. Sue and I sat on the couch patting Marvin and watching them.

"I don't really know how to dance," Sue said. "Do you?"

"Not that much." I was relieved. "I guess it's not so hard, though. Once you learn."

"Yeah." She passed me the popcorn and we sat there eating it.

"Come on, you guys," Angela shouted to us.

"Well, Annie, want to try?" Sue jumped up.

"Sure, I guess." I stood up carefully, smoothing my nightgown down.

Sue started waving her arms around. Then she dropped them. "I'm embarrassed," she said.

"Me, too. Besides, I have this dumb nightgown." I moved my feet a little bit. "It gets in the way."

"It looks neat, though," Sue said right away. "No kidding, Annie. It looks terrific on you, I think." She bent her knees and stepped back and forth in time to the beat. The music was very loud. "It makes you look older," Sue shouted over it. "I can sort of imagine how you'll look when you're sixteen or something."

"Really?" I took a bigger step and tried to move my arms like Kate and Janie. "I can't even imagine being *thirteen!*"

"I know it." Sue stopped jumping around. "Still, I guess it's not all that different. Look at Kate."

It was true. Except for the pierced ears, and the dancing, Kate seemed about the same. "Yeah. You don't have to change overnight or anything," I said.

All of a sudden, I got the feeling of how you move when you dance. It just seemed to come to me. The gown swirled around my legs. I was doing it!

"Look at me!" I yelled, and right then I lost my balance and tripped over the big chair and fell into it. I just lay there, laughing so hard I couldn't move. Angela tried to pull me up but then *she* fell onto the couch. Pretty soon everyone had flopped down somewhere. The record stopped.

"What time is it, anyway?" Janie asked.

Kate looked. It was three fifteen!

So we crept through the house to use the bathrooms, whispering and giggling and trying to keep Marvin quiet. Kate turned out the living-room lights. It was an awful mess in there, with the empty soda cans and spilled popcorn and the furniture pushed all around. I didn't know what Mrs. Levy would think in the morning. Probably she expected it, from a teenage kind of party.

Finally we went to the playroom and got settled on the couch and cots and sleeping bags down there. I had a rickety cot between Sue and Debbie that squeaked when I moved. Debbie said it was too much for her sensitive ears, but that was a joke. She conked out after about three minutes. She sleeps with her mouth open and snores a little. I wouldn't have expected it.

I rolled over and said "good night" to see if anyone would answer. Sue did.

"Listen, Annie, why don't you come over some day next week and we'll practice dancing."

"Neat." Then I remembered Rachel. But after all, I didn't need to see Rachel every day. I'd see her tomorrow to tell her all about the party. It was really too bad she had missed it. In the end, it turned out to be about the best party I ever went to.

7

Nora ran out yipping when I came home the next day. She acted as though I'd been gone on a long trip. In a way it seemed as though I had.

"Hi, sweetie!" I squatted down to hug her. She wasn't wheezing at all. She looked perfectly fine. I guess I sometimes worry too much.

"Have a good time?" Mom asked when I went inside.

"Yeah. Neat."

"I bet you stayed up till all hours."

"Yeah."

"How was your nightgown?"

"Good."

Mom looked sort of hurt. She probably expected me to tell her all about the party. It's hard to describe something like that to your mother without going into a whole complicated story. I just didn't feel like it. But

I felt a little sorry for Mom. I probably don't tell her stuff as much as I used to when I was younger.

"All the kids said the nightgown was neat," I said. "Thanks for letting me get it."

Mom gave me a quick hug. "You're welcome. I'm glad it was a success." She didn't ask any more questions. I think she's trying to be more tactful.

"Where's Kenny and Dad?" I asked.

"Kenny went off on a bike ride with Peter," Mom said. "Dad's working in the garden. Why don't you go up and get some sleep?"

I did feel pretty tired. "Well, maybe I'll take a little nap. Come on, Nora, want to go with me?"

Nora followed me up the steps with her tail thumping against the bannister. I got undressed and lay down, and she jumped up and settled down around my feet. I nudged her gently with my toes, and she sighed and went right off to sleep. Pretty soon I did, too.

After a while I heard the phone ring and Mom called me. It seemed as though I'd only been sleeping a few minutes, but the clock said six thirty! Nora was still curled up at the foot of the bed. I got out carefully so I wouldn't disturb her and went to the phone.

"Hi," Rachel said.

"Oh, hi, Rach!" I was awfully glad to hear her. "Do I sound funny? I've been asleep all afternoon. We didn't go to bed last night at Kate's till about three A.M.! You should have been there, Rach. It was such a neat party!" Then I remembered. "How was it, in the city?" I shouldn't have started right in about the party like that.

"It was good!" Rachel sounded more enthusiastic than I'd expected. "Guess what? I went to visit Barclay!"

"I didn't know you were going to do that!"

"I didn't either. Mom just called them up and they said to come over. School was out, but the director took us around. They have a big photography lab, Annie! The library's about twice as big as Schuyler's. And the classrooms were neat—they had rugs and pillows and couches, like real rooms. I'd be in Ms. Proctor's class, and the director says Ms. Proctor's one of the best teachers."

"Do you think you'll *go* there?" I was still sort of fuzzy from my nap. I couldn't take in what she was saying.

"Well, I'm applying."

"It seems so sudden!" My mouth tasted horrible.

"Everything's sudden," Rachel said. "Mom and Dad, moving—everything." She paused. "Anyway, seeing Barclay sort of helps me get used to the idea of moving. You know. I can see in some ways it might not be all bad."

"*I* wouldn't move somewhere just for a school!"

"Annie! I don't *want* to move, I *have* to. I'm just saying at least the school part of it might be good, that's all. I should think you'd be glad for me."

"I am," I said quickly. I *was,* I guess. But it was awful to wake up from a nap and have Rachel be all excited about going to some city school. I wasn't ready. I wished she would ask me about the party. There was so much to tell.

"Anyway, that's not all," Rachel went right on. "I met these kids Aunt Sylvia knows, who go to Barclay. Erica and Bruce. They were so nice, Annie! They weren't stuck-up or anything. They told me a lot of stuff about Barclay. They both really like it. Bruce is on the soccer team. Soccer's their big sport. Bruce sort of reminded me of Kenny."

"Did he look like Frankenstein?"

"Annie! I mean, he's fourteen, and he's friendly."

I decided to let that go. It was Erica I was worrying about. "How old is Erica?"

"Thirteen. You should see her—she has straight blond hair almost down to her waist!"

I wasn't sure I wanted to see her. I shifted the phone to my other ear and sat down on Mom's bed. It looked as though Rachel was going to go on and on.

"Bruce had to go somewhere, but Erica took me all over the neighborhood. We went to Central Park, and to some little shops and a neat ice-cream place. Erica only lives a block from Aunt Sylvia. It was neat going around with her."

"Oh." If Rachel moved near there, they'd probably get very friendly. They sounded pretty friendly already.

"You should hear the things Bruce and Erica do! They go all over the city to rock concerts and movies and museums and stuff. Erica says there's a party every month at Barclay. She says the kids who go there are really friendly and nice. It's a very integrated school—they even have kids from Japan, and Africa. It's not like Schuyler, where everybody's the same."

It's true that Madison is the kind of mostly white suburb that people write snotty magazine articles about. Those articles always make me mad. *I* didn't ask my town to be the way it is. I'd like it to be more integrated. Now Rachel was sounding like the articles.

"Everyone's *not* the same here," I argued. "Just because you're the same color, that doesn't make you identical!" I suddenly remembered how we used to want to be twins. "I'm not the same as *you,* even," I said.

"I know *that,*" Rachel said quickly. "*You*'re the lucky one. *You* have this simple, perfect life with your perfect parents and your brother and your dog—" She sort of laughed. "Too bad Nora isn't called Spot, then you'd be as perfect as the family in those dumb Dick and Jane books!"

"Hey, Rach!" That was mean. It hurt my feelings.

"I'm sorry," Rachel said right away. "I'm sorry, Annie." She hesitated. "Oh," she said. "I didn't even ask you about the party. How was it?"

"It was neat!" It was hard to get as enthusiastic as

I'd been before. I tried to think of the most interesting part. "Debbie was there," I said.

"Debbie *Gold*stein?"

I knew that would get her! "She was pretty nice, actually," I said. "She has a very good sense of humor, once she gets going. You should have heard some of the crazy things she said!"

"Like what?"

"Oh, I don't know." I was still feeling hurt. "It probably wouldn't sound that funny if I told you now. You had to *be* there."

"Sure," Rachel said in a subdued tone. "I wish I had been. I guess you all had a pretty good time."

"Oh, it was terrific!" I said. "We were dancing and everything!" I waited for her reaction.

"Since when do *you* know how to dance?" Rachel asked quickly.

"Well, I don't, but Sue and I started to because everyone else was, and it was pretty easy, really, once we got the hang of it. Anyway, we're going to practice together this week so we'll be experts pretty soon—" I stopped. I probably shouldn't have said that. I wished I hadn't.

"Oh," Rachel said. "Well, I guess I better get off the phone. Dad's going back to the city soon."

"Rach—" I said. "Listen, Rach, I really missed you at the party." That was true. Why hadn't I said it right off? "Anyway," I stumbled on. "I'll stop by for you tomorrow, O.K.?"

"Sure," Rachel said.

After we had hung up I stood by the phone feeling miserable. I didn't know how I would face Rachel in the morning.

But when she came to her door all I could think of was how glad I was to see her.

"Hi," she said, almost shyly. She was wearing a new red T-shirt with *NEW YORK* across the front in white letters. Her figure looked quite nice under it. She looked older.

"Oh, hi, Rach!" I said. "Where'd you get that shirt? It's neat!"

"At this place near Aunt Sylvia's," she said. She didn't mention going with Erica. I could tell she wanted to get back to normal as much as I did. "Want to see what else I got, for the doll house?" She turned back to the hall table and held up a little tiny pot with a baby cactus in it.

"Oh, Rach, it's so cute! I never thought of having live plants in the doll house. Where will you put it—on the dining-room table?"

"There, or it could go on the mantel," Rachel said, putting the pot down. She came outside and slammed her front door shut. "I was thinking, we could make little hanging planters for the kitchen, too," she went on as we started down her walk.

"That's a neat idea!" I was so glad she'd brought up the doll house. It felt nice to make plans for it again. It seemed like a long time since we had. "Maybe we could dig up some little plants from your yard," I said enthusiastically. "We could use doll dishes for planters. Want to start this afternoon?"

"I can't. I'm going to the eye doctor. Mom wants me to see him before we move."

"Oh." Just her mentioning moving made me uncomfortable again. "Well, some day soon, anyway," I said.

We walked on for a while without talking. All the yards were green. The trees had soft little leaves on them. Spring's always my favorite season. But this spring was so different.

"Hey, Annie! Rachel! Wait up!"

Sue ran across the street. Any other time I would have been glad to see her, but now I tensed up. I just knew she'd bring up the party.

"We missed you at the party, Rachel!" she said right away. "Did Annie tell you about it?"

"A little," Rachel said. I could feel her tensing up, too.

"You should have seen us all dancing," Sue went on, "right, Annie?"

"Yeah," I said uncomfortably. I didn't know how to stop her. Sue's so enthusiastic about everything.

"I guess you wouldn't really call it dancing," she went on. "It was more bumping around to music! But it was fun."

The next thing, she'd bring up my coming over. I knew it.

"Annie's coming over to practice with me some day," she said cheerfully, before I could think how to stop her. But then she went right on. "You come, too, Rachel. Want to?"

I was so relieved! I shouldn't have worried. Sue's too nice to hurt someone's feelings on purpose.

Rachel only hesitated a minute. "Sure, that would be good," she said. "Anyway, I have to start learning. Because I'm going to move to the city and go to this school where they have parties and everything. Probably all of them know how to dance."

"You're *moving*? Sue was startled. "Oh, Rachel—I'll *miss* you! How come?"

"My parents are getting a divorce," Rachel said straightforwardly. She must have decided to tell people. In a way, I was glad. It's worse when you try to hide something like that.

"Oh, wow—that's too bad," Sue said quickly. "That's tough, Rachel." She knows. Her parents broke up when she was little. "I'm sorry," she said, touching Rachel's arm. "How are you doing?"

"I'll be O.K.," Rachel said. "Once I get used to it."

"Yeah. You will, Rachel. It's hard, though. And moving, too—"

"She'll make friends in the city, though," I said. "She's already met some kids."

Rachel looked at me gratefully. I was really glad I had said it.

We crossed into the block school was on. The sidewalks were filling up with kids and buses turned into the driveways. Someone ran up behind us and said, "Hi!" We turned. It was Debbie. I was surprised how glad I was to see her. Going to a party with someone can make a big difference.

"That's a neat shirt, Rachel," Debbie said right away. "Hey, you missed a great party!"

Then Janie and Kate ran up. Kate was wearing Rachel's necklace. She started thanking her. Everybody began to tell Rachel about the party and say they'd missed her. Rachel looked more relaxed.

"Boy," she said, sounding like her regular self. "I don't know about you guys—the minute my back is turned—"

Debbie started to tell her about my nightgown.

I saw Alan Shay and Tony Albrecht walking over. "Shut *up!*" I yelled, poking her. "They'll *hear* you!"

Everyone laughed. Rachel was laughing too.

I suddenly began to feel good. It was fun to stand there kidding around with everyone. It's neat to have a whole gang of friends.

Then the bell rang. Rachel and I put our arms around each other and walked up the steps in step, the way we always did. I was glad the day had started out so well.

But it ended up being one of the most terrible days of my life.

It was the day Nora died.

8

It started to rain in sixth period and when school let out it was still raining, so I stayed after to work in the library. When the rain slowed down to a drizzle, I went home.

Nora didn't run out to meet me when I got there. I don't know why I didn't realize something was wrong, right then. Maybe I thought she was just sleeping. I don't know.

There was a note from Mom saying she'd gone to the print shop and Kenny would be home late. She asked me to start dinner. I took the lamb chops out of the fridge and peeled some carrots and cut them up and started washing lettuce for a salad. I was patting the lettuce dry in a dish towel when I suddenly missed Nora.

I don't know how to explain it, but at that exact minute, with the damp lettuce in the towel in my hands, I *knew*. I knew something was terribly wrong. Before I even called her.

I tried to squash the feeling down. I started to look for Nora in her favorite sleeping places: the chair she wasn't supposed to lie in, the hall rug, the foot of my bed, Kenny's closet floor.

"Nora!" I called. "Where are you, honey?"

She wasn't anywhere in the house.

So I ran outside, calling as loud as I could. "Nora! *Nora!* Come on, Nora. Please!"

The rain had stopped, but everything was soaked. She'd be in some sheltered place. I looked under the back porch and inside the garage and under the row of evergreens at the edge of the vegetable garden. I ran to the front of the house and looked under the steps and around to the side where the roof hangs out and makes a dry place. She wasn't there.

Then I knew where she had to be. I went toward it, feeling dizzy with fear as I got closer. I called in a softer voice so I wouldn't frighten her. "Nora, are you there? Here I am, Nora. I'm coming."

And she was there—under the lilac bush, curled up into a little mound of damp fur on the wet grass with rain dripping onto her from the lilac flowers. Her tail thumped weakly as I crawled under the wet branches to reach her. Her eyes were open. She looked at me in such a sad way as she tried to inch toward me. Her legs twitched and her tail thumped pitifully and she gave a sharp little moan. Then she began to wheeze.

This wheezing was different, deep and dry. Her whole body trembled when she did it.

"Oh, Nora," I whispered. "Oh, you poor thing!"

I touched her head softly and smoothed my hand down her back as gently as I could. I felt weak from the smell of the lilacs and the chill of the ground and the sight of Nora's stomach swelling out with every wheeze. I wanted to hold her tight so she couldn't wheeze any more. I wanted to carry her to some warm dry place. But I know you aren't supposed to move anyone who's that sick. So I just scrunched down on the wet ground with my head next to hers and put my arm around her and lay there and stroked her while she trembled and wheezed. I know she was glad I was with her. I could tell.

It felt as though we were there for hours but I guess it was only about ten minutes. It was the most awful ten minutes of my whole life. It was so lonely. I wished Mom or Kenny would come back home. The branches dripped, and the ground was so cold. Nora's eyes were dark and far away. I always used to wonder how people know when someone's dying. You can tell. You see it in their eyes. Nora wheezed again, yelping afterward as her body jerked. She was so little and thin! She looked almost like a puppy. I put my face against her wet fur. "I love you, Nora," I said. "I love you so much!"

Nora wheezed again, more quietly this time. "It's O.K., Nora," I comforted her. "You're going to be

O.K." But I knew it wasn't true. She raised her head a little bit and laid it closer to mine so that our eyes looked into each other's. Then, thumping her tail softly as though she was trying to please me by doing a trick just right, she gave a little quick gasp, and died.

Her body twitched and went still. I tried to hear her heart, but there was no sound. "Nora!" I cried, hugging her close. "Oh, Nora, I'm going to miss you so much!" I missed her terribly already.

I took her into my arms very carefully and crawled slowly out of the lilacs. Branches scraped against my face. I carried her to the house and set her down in the old sling chair on the back porch. Then I ran upstairs for something to cover her with. In the linen closet I found the big beach towel with black and honey stripes. The honey was exactly the same color as Nora's fur. Once I used that towel for Nora after a bath and Mom got mad, but I knew she wouldn't be mad now. I was carrying the towel downstairs when the word "shroud" came into my head. It has such a sad, heavy sound. All at once I started to cry. I pressed the shroud against my face and cried and cried and cried.

Mom came in the front door. "Annie! What's wrong, hon?"

She grabbed me in a hug with the towel bunched up between us. "What *is* it? What's happened?"

It felt so good to be in her arms. "It's Nora!" I sobbed out. "Nora's *dead*."

"Oh, Annie, are you sure?" Mom hugged me

tighter. "Oh, how terrible I wasn't here." She was crying, too. "Where is she?"

I took her out to the back porch where Nora lay. Mom squatted down beside the chair and listened for her heart. "Oh, Annie," she said. "Oh, I'm so sorry!"

I patted the towel around Nora's soft, thin little body.

"I couldn't do anything, Mom! She just lay there wheezing so pitifully, and I couldn't do anything for her!"

Mom wiped my eyes with a corner of the towel. "Just being with her was the best thing you could do, hon. Giving her love."

I looked down. "I can't get used to the idea. That she's dead."

Kenny ran up the steps and stopped when he saw us. "What happened?"

"Nora died." I said it quickly, before Mom could. It seemed like my responsibility to say it.

"Oh, man." Kenny squatted down beside the chair. "Poor old dog. Poor Nora." He patted her head softly. "The hair on her ear's all tangled," he said. Very gently, he worked the tangle out.

The front door slammed and Mom ran into the house. I heard her talking to Dad. He came out to the porch and hugged me.

"I'm sorry, Coke." He bent down and touched Nora gently. "I'm going to miss her," he said. "She was a good old dog."

"We'll miss her so *much!*" I said. Suddenly I turned on Dad. "If only you'd taken her to the vet that night! I told you she might be sick, but you wouldn't listen."

Dad stroked my hair. "I'm sorry, Coke."

"It's too late to be sorry!" I yelled. "It's too late—she's *dead!*"

Dad held me tighter, but he didn't say anything. I knew he felt terrible. He loved Nora. He didn't want her to die. Suddenly, my anger faded. But my sorrow swelled up again. "It's not your fault," I said, putting my arms around him for comfort. "She's just dead, that's all."

"I'm sorry we didn't take her to the vet," Dad said soberly. "Medicine might have helped her. But she was an old dog. She had come to the end of her life." He squeezed me. "She had a long, happy life."

"I know it." In my head I pictured Nora running across our yard after a squirrel. "She was such a fast runner!" I said.

Kenny laughed. "Remember the time she ran off with that little kid's cone at the Dairy Queen?"

I had to laugh too, remembering. "And the time she buried her bone in the vegetable garden and dug up a whole row of cauliflowers looking for it!"

"I won't forget *that,*" Dad said.

"She was a dumb old dog," Kenny said lovingly.

"She was smart!" I said quickly. "She was the smartest dog in the world!"

"The nicest, anyway," said Mom. "There could

never be a dog as sweet and loving as she was." The way she said it, it was like a blessing.

After dinner I had to call Rachel. It was so awful to keep having to tell people. I was almost too choked up to talk, but Rachel began to cry so I guess she heard me. I asked her to come over right away to see Nora before we buried her. Dad had said we had to do it that night, before her body stiffened and changed.

Rachel came with a bunch of tulips for Nora's grave. I was awfully glad to see her. She was the only person outside my family who knew how much I had loved Nora.

"I'm really sorry, Annie," she said. She was crying.

"I know it, Rach. Thanks." Then I cried some more.

We buried Nora under the lilacs. We all took turns digging the hole. Dad arranged Nora's box in it, and Rachel and I covered the box and smoothed the dirt over it with our hands. Rachel put the tulips there, and I put the fresh lilacs I'd cut. Then Kenny pulled something out of his pocket and handed it to me. It was a small piece of polished wood. He'd burned *NORA, 1969–1979* into it with his woodburning kit.

"It's to mark her grave," he said.

"Oh, Kenny, it's beautiful," I said. Sometimes I just love Kenny.

We set the marker on top of the grave, in the fresh dirt. I couldn't believe that *Nora* was lying under that dirt. She would never see what Kenny had made for her. All of a sudden I began to sob. Rachel put her arm around me.

Dad said, "Remember that book we used to read when you were little, *The Dead Bird*?"

I nodded.

"There's a page at the end, after the children have buried the bird, with a picture of all of them flying their kites. And the words say, 'And every day, until they forgot, they went back to their little dead bird and put fresh flowers on its grave.'"

"I'll *never* forget!"

"You'll never forget Nora," Dad said. "None of us will. But each day the sadness of her death will fade away a little."

I couldn't believe it. I didn't want to believe it yet. But I understood what he meant.

"Thanks," I said. I put my head against his chest and hugged him hard.

That was Nora's funeral.

9

Spring got more beautiful each day. The trees were a soft green and Mom's iris were blooming and all the air smelled sweet. The least little thing could make me cry. A dog running across a yard. A sad part in a book. A loving glance from Mom. A dog-food ad on television. A couple of times I cried when Rachel tried to make me laugh, because I was so grateful to her.

I missed Nora terribly.

Nothing I did seemed real. I felt as though I was a stranger who was pretending to be Annie Morrison, a girl whose dog had died just when her best friend was moving away and her whole life seemed to be changing. It was almost like being in a play about this girl, without knowing how she should act or what lines she was supposed to say. Or what was going to happen to her in the next scene.

I kept wondering when the sadness would fade. It

was still so sharp my throat ached. Every day when I came home from school I had to stop myself from wishing Nora would run out the door and jump down the steps and throw herself at me with her tail thumping happily against my legs.

One afternoon as I was walking slowly up the driveway, Peter James came up behind me and tapped my shoulder.

"Oh, hi!" I was startled. "Hi, Peter." I hadn't seen him since Nora died. I'd been trying not to bump into him. Now I felt awkward and shy.

"I just wanted to say I'm sorry about Nora."

"Oh. Thanks. Thanks a lot." I stood there dumbly. I didn't know what to say. I was ashamed to talk about dying with Peter. I would have hated him to think I was stupid to be heartbroken over just a dog, when having your father die must be about a million times worse.

"I really miss her," Peter said. "She was such a good old dog. It's funny to come by your house and not have her run out with her tail wagging."

"I know it! That's how I feel, whenever I come home," I said. "It's so hard to get used to the idea that she's *dead!*" As soon as I said that I wished I hadn't. What Peter had to get used to was so very much worse.

But he didn't act offended. He nodded seriously. "It's a tough thing to get used to," he said. He stood there for a minute, looking at me thoughtfully as though we shared the same experience, even though all I knew of death was Nora. I thought that was awfully kind of him. He reached out and touched my arm. "I'm really sorry," he said. Then he turned and walked away.

"Thanks, Peter," I called after him. I realized I had felt more comfortable with Peter just then, talking about *dying,* than I ever had before, when I was worrying about making pointless conversation or wondering how I looked. I think Peter's own sorrow must make him sympathetic to other people. I hope I can get to be more like that.

Mom wasn't home that afternoon. The house seemed very empty. I made a snack and changed my clothes and went to the basement to take clean sheets for my bed from the drier. I was pulling them out when I looked up and saw Nora's dog-chow dish on the back of a shelf where Mom must have put it, not wanting to throw it away but knowing I wasn't ready to think of another dog. When I saw the dish, I burst out crying, wiping my face on a warm clean sheet. Then I ran back upstairs and threw myself down on my bed with the sun pouring across my legs and cried and cried until I fell asleep.

Later that afternoon I got my first period.

Of course, it wasn't a surprise. I had always known it would happen. But I think I probably never truly believed it until it did. Knowing about something ahead of time doesn't help you that much. You could talk about it with your mother and see movies about it in school and read millions of ads about girls climbing mountains or drinking Cokes while they're having their periods and still not really know how you'll feel when it finally happens to you. The ads say you feel "carefree." But how could anyone be carefree when they're noticing shifts and rumblings going on inside them and seeing this bloody stuff come out of them? Or feel carefree about the stuff getting your period is supposed to mean you're ready for, when you know you're not ready yet. And you aren't sure you ever want to be. I certainly didn't feel carefree about all that. I felt strange.

But at the same time, I was relieved. I must have been worried about getting my period for a long time without ever actually admitting it to myself. I think it made me tense. It's probably one reason I used to be so bothered by kids like Debbie or Iris McGee acting sophisticated. Maybe it's why I never especially wanted to bring up the subject with Rachel. I didn't like her to know how uncomfortable it made me. Now that it had finally happened, I wouldn't need to worry about it all the time. I could relax. That was the good part.

The bad part was that I didn't know how to tell Rachel. It wasn't that I wanted to keep it from her, but for some reason it was hard to just come right out and say it: "I got my period." Telling Mom was more natural, somehow. I knew beforehand that Mom would be pleased. I didn't know how Rachel would feel about it.

For days after it happened, I couldn't seem to tell her. Whenever I planned to, it would turn out that Rachel had to go somewhere, or we'd be with other kids, or we would finally be alone and then I'd be too shy to bring it up. But I had to tell her. She'd find out sometime, and she'd be hurt to discover I hadn't told her right away. Finally, I promised myself that the next time we were by ourselves I'd just come out and say it.

The next time would be Saturday. Rachel wasn't going to the city. She wanted me to walk around Madison with her so she could take pictures of me in all our familiar places for her album. I was a little embarrassed—I told her I'd feel like Annie Morrison, Girl of Suburbia—but I was glad she wanted to do it.

On Saturday morning I put on my nicest shirt and brushed my hair especially well. I knew Rachel wouldn't let me brush it later. Real photographers like Rachel and her father don't want you to look as though you've gotten ready for the camera. All Mr. Weiss's photographs of Rachel have her with messy hair or dirty bare feet or milk on her mouth. They're good pictures, though. They look just like her.

I arranged my hair carefully and then I messed it up just a little so it wouldn't *look* arranged. I tucked my shirt tighter and stared at myself in the mirror. My breasts seemed to look as though they belonged there. Maybe it was just that I was getting more used to them. After all, I had got my period, too.

Kenny was sleeping late, but Mom and Dad were in the kitchen when I went down.

Mom looked at me approvingly, and gave me a hug. "Good morning!" she said.

"You look very pretty this morning, Coke," said Dad.

I think they're both pleased that I'm growing up.

When I got to Rachel's, Mrs. Weiss was just backing out of the garage.

"Hi, Annie," she said. "Isn't it a beautiful day? I'm so glad you and Rachel can spend it together." She looked at me lovingly. "How *are* you these days? You must really miss that beautiful dog of yours."

"I do," I said. "I'm O.K. It's just hard to get used to it." I suddenly wanted to say something comforting to her. "How are *you*?" I asked. "I hope you're O.K., as much as you can be."

Mrs. Weiss reached out of the car window and touched my cheek. "Thank you, hon. It'll take a while, I guess, but I'll be fine." She smiled and blew me a kiss and drove away.

"Stay there!" Rachel ran out of the house and took a picture of me coming up the walk. Then we went inside and she took me beside the doll house. After that, we started downtown.

It was about ten in the morning. The sun was already high and almost hot. The yards on Rachel's street were dappled with leaf shadows. We walked along slowly without saying much. I thought of what I was going to tell Rachel. I didn't have to do it right away.

We turned onto Main Street at the post-office corner and went past the barber shop and the stationery store. For a joke, Rachel took my picture by the window of a store that sells fat ladies' clothes. A warm sugary smell was pouring out of the doughnut shop next door.

"Let's get doughnuts," Rachel said. She pronounced it "do-nuts" because that's how the sign is spelled. Once, when we were in about third grade, Rachel tried to complain about the spelling, but the woman behind the counter didn't understand her. She called the cook out, and he patted Rachel's head and gave us each a free jelly doughnut. So it was worthwhile, but they never changed the sign.

We bought our doughnuts and took them outside. Rachel finished hers quickly and wiped her hands.

"Hold that bite!" She put her camera to her eye.

"Rach—I'm all sticky!" I wiped at my chin and tried to look dignified.

Rachel snapped my picture. "Let's go to the bookstore," she said.

We must have been there hundreds of times, from way back before we could read. It's a good bookstore. They let you browse. We headed for the paperback rack in the side room and twirled it around to see what was new.

"Hey, remember this?" I stopped the rack and took down *Ramona the Pest.*

Rachel grabbed it from me. "Is this the one where the TV announcer scolds her?" She began to flip through the pages.

"Rachel! I got it first!"

She laughed. "You sound the way you used to in the third grade!"

"You *act* like it! Come on, let's read it together."

We stood there laughing over the book. On every page there was something we remembered. It's strange how the look and feel of a book can take you back in time.

Rachel took my picture in front of the book rack. Then she suddenly reached up and pulled out another book. It was *Now and Forever.*

"Erica says this is one of the best books she ever read," she said. "She says John Paul Marsten really understands the way kids feel. I'm glad I saw this—I'm going to get it."

I stopped myself from making a quick remark. Maybe it *was* a good book. If Rachel liked it, I could borrow it from her. You can probably learn a lot from a book like that. I had a lot to learn. I suddenly remembered what I was going to tell Rachel. "Let's go to Woolworth's," I said, to put it off.

We always love to browse around in there. For years our favorite place was the toy section, where we'd pore over jacks sets and play money and doll furniture. We still sometimes sneak down that aisle to buy rubber monsters and wind-up cars for each other for Christmas stockings.

Rachel wanted me to pose on the bucking-bronco ride outside the store, but I talked her out of that. We went inside, and I let her take my picture at the toy counter with a Little Kiddie Doctor bag in my hand. But then some real little kids came along and I was embarrassed.

"Hey, Rachel—let's do the photo booth!" We love to go in there and take crazy pictures of ourselves. We have a whole collection of them.

We ran over to the photo booth and pulled the curtain and put our money in and posed. We did a normal pose first and then we made a face. Real fast, we changed the pose and leaned back languidly like movie stars. Then Rachel pretended to take a picture with her camera. When the pictures came out, the movie-star one was pretty good.

"We ought to make a whole set of these," Rachel said. "In all different glamorous poses."

"We should have makeup—lipstick and stuff."

"Let's go buy some!" Rachel said right away.

So we went over to the makeup counter and picked out a dark red lipstick and some black mascara and took it back into the photo booth. We pulled the curtain shut and began to make each other up, watching ourselves in the mirror and giggling. When we made smudges, we used Rachel's lens tissue to wipe them off. We were cracking up the whole time, but when we had finished we sat back and stared at ourselves in the mirror in amazement. We looked about ten years older, and quite beautiful.

Rachel put in the money, and the camera began to click. We didn't make faces. We stared straight at the mirror and let the camera take us the way we were. The way we might get to be.

"Rachel," I said suddenly, before the last click, "I got my period."

"Oh, Annie!" Rachel turned in surprise, blurring the picture that came out a minute later. "So did I!"

We grabbed each other and hung on, laughing. I guess we probably never felt more identical to each other in our lives than we did just then. Just then, when we were going to have to part.

10

Probably anyone who saw us waiting for the New York bus the next Saturday would have thought we were just two girls going to the city for fun. But it was more complicated than that. I felt nervous about the trip. I knew it would make Rachel's move seem more real. I was afraid of acting stupid because I didn't know my way around New York City that well. I was shy about meeting Erica and Bruce, which was part of the plan. And then—it was the first time Rachel and I were going somewhere since we'd *told* each other. I think it made us both feel a little awkward, the way people do when they wish they could change the subject but don't know how.

We stood in the shade of the post-office building and looked up the street for the bus, without saying much. Two women were waiting there with us. They had pants suits and handbags and beauty-shop hair-dos.

"Going to the city, girls?" one of them asked.

"Yeah," I admitted. I hoped she wasn't going to try to take *care* of us.

"Well, it's the perfect day for it!" She patted her hairdo. "Now yesterday, that was something awful, the way it rained—"

Luckily, the bus came just then. Rachel and I settled into a seat. Rachel took out her camera. I checked my bag to be sure I had everything—money, hairbrush, the subway map Mom had made me take. I'd die before I'd use it in front of anyone, but if I got lost I could go into a toilet somewhere and lock the door and look at it.

The bus drove past the bank and the drugstore and Memorial Park. Madison looks different when you're riding through it on your way somewhere. I wondered if Rachel already thought of it as where she used to live. After a while we turned onto the highway. I leaned back and watched the scruffy woods and industrial parks and shopping centers go by. We passed an office building, and I read the words on a window without really thinking. Then I looked again, and started laughing.

"Hey, Rach—did you see that sign? It said 'Stephen Berger, Attorney,' but there was a big space between the *p* and the *h!*"

"What's funny about that?"

"Step-hen!" I explained. "Get it? Step-hen Berger, Attorney! Like, Order in the court, the *chicken* wants to speak, cluck, cluck, cluck!"

Rachel began to laugh, and pretty soon neither one of us could stop. We were practically hysterical. My bag slipped down, and when I leaned over to get it I hit my head on the seat in front of me. Rachel howled. I howled, too, even though it hurt. I laughed so hard I thought I might throw up.

But then the bus stopped for a crowd of people, and we drove around a ramp and onto the bridge. Rachel leaned over, held up her camera, and snapped. "I can't believe I'm going to live there," she said. She stopped laughing, and so did I.

We followed the crowd through the bus station and down to the subway platform. The women from Madison were there. They didn't seem to fit anywhere—in Madison you could tell they were going somewhere and here you knew they'd come from somewhere. I felt sort of sorry for them.

The train came in, and we got on. Rachel leaned back and shut her eyes. I kept mine open and read the advertisements while the train lurched downtown, screeching around the curves. At 125th Street a bunch of black girls with Afros and high wedge shoes burst on and grabbed straps above us. They were shouting and kidding around about one girl's boy friend. I felt self-conscious sitting under them. I wondered if they guessed I came from the suburbs.

The train slowed, and Rachel opened her eyes. "Here's our stop," she said, without even looking out to check. I followed her up some steps and through the turnstile and out to the bright street. It was crowded with people. A man was selling neckties from a suitcase.

"This way." Rachel started off around him.

I hurried after her. "I don't see how you know."

"You just do," she said vaguely, pushing through an opening in the crowd.

I pressed after her, but two men with briefcases got between us so I couldn't see her. For a minute I was afraid I might get lost. Then I looked up and saw her bending over a pushcart at the corner.

"Ices!" she said when I caught up to her. "My father says New York is the only place in the world besides Rome, Italy, where you can get a decent Italian ice." She handed me a little paper cup.

"Where's the spoon?"

"You don't *need* a spoon, dope. You lick from the top and push up from the bottom."

"Oh." I knew it. We'd hardly even started, and already I felt stupid.

We crossed the avenue with hundreds of other people while cars honked and a taxi cut right in front of us. The bus exhaust smelled awful. I don't know how people stand it. I concentrated on keeping up with Rachel. We got to the corner, and I looked up and recognized the museum block.

"The museum's down there." Rachel pointed.

"I *know* it." She's not the only person who's been to the Museum of Modern Art. I was there two different times before, with my family.

Still, it was much neater to be there with Rachel. I love the museum. It makes you feel very dramatic to walk through the big white rooms with your heels clicking on the stone floors and look at paintings. Seeing a painting in person is much better than just seeing a picture of it. It's more real. You think about the actual person who brushed the paint on.

Rachel and I walked through the rooms slowly, stopping whenever we felt like it. When we came out into the lobby again we went upstairs to see a photography exhibition. Rachel studied the photographs carefully one by one with her glasses right up near the frames. I watched her, feeling sort of jealous. It must be wonderful to know what you want to do, from the beginning, like her. She's planned to be a photographer since about first grade. I just started thinking about being a writer this year.

"Someday I bet I'll come here and see a show of yours," I said.

Rachel turned around. "Don't be stupid. I'd never be that good."

"You're good now. I think you're very good, honestly I do."

"That's different," Rachel said intensely, pushing her glasses back. "That's *nothing*."

She acted as though my compliment didn't count. Well, I may not be some great critic, but at least I can have my own opinion. I know what I like. I suddenly had the feeling I might cry.

Rachel touched my arm. "Thanks anyway, though." Maybe she could tell. "Let's go eat."

We got tuna salad sandwiches and iced tea in the cafeteria and carried our trays out to the sculpture garden. It's a very sophisticated place to eat lunch, but I didn't feel sophisticated. I stirred my tea and watched people looking at the statues. In back of Rachel a bald-headed man was taking pictures of a huge nude statue of a woman. He was pretty funny, but I didn't have the energy to start laughing with Rachel. Maybe sometime I could tell Debbie about it. And Sue. I'd describe how the man walked around and around, snapping the statue from all angles. They'd probably crack up.

"What's funny?" Rachel asked.

"Nothing."

"Oh." Rachel drained her iced tea. "Want to go buy some postcards?"

We went into the store and browsed through the racks. I got a card of a Chagall painting for my bulletin board. I picked out cards for Mom and Dad and

Kenny. Then I saw a card with a scene of two people dancing, from a 1930's movie. It would be perfect for Sue.

"Look!" I showed it to Rachel. "I'm going to get this for Sue. Isn't it good?"

"Yeah." She turned away quickly and started looking at books. I pretended to look through the posters but I couldn't concentrate. After a few minutes I went over and tapped her shoulder.

"Maybe we should go, so we have time for the jeans store."

"Oh. Yeah." Rachel closed the book slowly. "This is the most fabulous book I ever saw" she said passionately.

It was *A History of American Photography*. "Are you going to get it?" I asked.

"I can't—it costs twenty-five dollars."

Suddenly I made the decision to get that book for Rach for a going-away present. It would be perfect! I'd ask Mom to order it. I could pay her back from my allowances. It was an awful lot of money, but Rachel deserved it. She'd really be pleased.

Getting that idea made me feel better. The sun was bright when we left the museum. It was a gorgeous day. The people on the street looked interesting. Rachel and I walked along slowly, staring into shop windows. I could see how people like living in New York. I was glad I was getting to know it better.

Rachel pulled my sleeve. "Here, we'll walk up Sixth Avenue."

I looked up at the sign above her head. "This is the Avenue of the Americas," I said.

"The Avenue of the Americas *is* Sixth Avenue," Rachel said impatiently. "Nobody but tourists calls it that."

That was so mean! I followed Rachel to the subway and we got on a train and rode uptown in silence. We got out on Broadway and 72nd Street. It's dirtier than 53rd. There are more people who look strange. I saw an old woman in a coat and bedroom slippers poking around in a trash can. Two men were sitting on a bench sharing a wine bottle. It was depressing.

Suddenly Rachel grabbed me. "Look!"

She pulled me toward a dress store with three dresses in the window—red, blue, and yellow—all the same style with puffed sleeves, drawstring necks, and wide skirts. They were terrific dresses.

"I bet they cost about a hundred dollars," I said.

"They might not!" Rachel said. "They have pockets," she added. We hate clothes without pockets. "We could ask how much they are," she said, tentatively.

"But, Rachel—you wanted *jeans!*" I said, to stop her from going in there and embarrassing us. Rachel never wears a dress.

"Can't I change my *mind?*" Rachel demanded. "Do you think you *own* my opinions or something?" She seemed so angry, suddenly, for no reason.

"No I *don't!*" I shouted, exasperated. "I don't understand you at all! This whole day you've been dragging me around like some big New York expert, making me feel stupid. It hurts my feelings!"

"I'm *sorry* if I hurt your *feelings*." Rachel leaned back against the store window. "I'm sorry if I made you waste your day going around with me when you could have been having a wonderful time in Madison with Sue, or Debbie *Gold*stein!"

"Yeah, well, I'm sorry you have to spend your time with me when you could be with *Erica!*" I said right back. A little kid with a baseball hat on was staring at us. I stared at him and he slid away. "That's who you probably *wish* you were with!"

"As a matter of fact, Erica has her acting class today."

"Oh, so *that's* why you asked me!"

"It's *not,* Annie. What's the matter with you?"

"I don't know." There was half a filthy pretzel by my foot. I kicked it. "It just seems like you're already a New Yorker," I said more quietly. "Probably when you start going to Barclay you'll get all these new friends—"

"*Annie!* Don't you even want me to *have* friends, when you're going to be back in Madison with everyone—" She looked at me defiantly. "I keep wondering who's going to be your new best friend."

"I'm not going to *have* a new best friend. *You're* my best friend!" I said angrily.

"Well, you're *my* best friend!" Rachel said furiously.

For a minute we stared at each other, while what we'd said sank in. Then we started laughing.

"As I was saying, before I was so rudely interrupted," Rachel said. "Want to go in and see how much those dresses cost?"

"Yeah." I opened the door for her and waved her in.

The saleswoman was standing right inside. I wondered if she'd heard us fighting, but she didn't say anything. Rachel asked her how much the dresses were, and the woman said they were eighteen dollars.

"That's just a couple more dollars than jeans!" I said to Rachel.

She nodded. I could see she wanted to get one, but she was sort of waiting for me.

"Do you have the blue in size eight?" I asked the woman.

"And the yellow?" Rachel said.

I held my breath while the woman hunted through a rack of dresses and pulled out the right ones. She took us to a dressing room. We took our jeans and shirts off and helped each other put on the dresses. They were quite long. I loved the way mine hung around my legs.

"You look terrific!" Rachel said.

"So do you!"

We giggled at each other in the mirror.

"Want to get them?" Rachel asked.

"Yeah," I said. I was sure Mom wouldn't mind.

She'd probably be *glad* I got something besides jeans.

"Want to *wear* them?" Rachel said.

"Sure!"

So we paid for the dresses, and the woman folded our old clothes into shopping bags. "Enjoy!" she said.

I felt a little shy walking out of the shop. I'm not that used to wearing a dress. I turned and began to walk self-consciously down the sidewalk.

"This way!" Rachel pulled me gently in the right direction.

I put my arm across her shoulders and we walked along in step. Probably anyone who saw us then thought we were both New York City girls.

11

"Look at *you!*" Rachel's Aunt Sylvia said at the door. "You look *terrific!* Where'd you get those dresses? I wouldn't mind having a dress like that."

"At this store on Broadway," I answered casually.

"Well, you both look marvelous. I bet you're exhausted, though. I made you some lemonade."

We went in and sank down on her couch and kicked our shoes off. It felt wonderful to sit down. Aunt Sylvia's apartment is neat. It's just the one room, plus a little kitchen and a bathroom. There isn't much furniture except for bookshelves. There are piles of books everywhere, including on the floor.

She gave us lemonade and sat down across from us, studying us over the rim of her glass. "You've changed, Annie! How long's it been since I've seen you—three or four months? You look so *good*. You both do." She paused. "It just takes a bit of getting used to, to think of you as adolescents."

It didn't bother me when Aunt Sylvia said that. For one thing, she's so matter-of-fact you don't get embarrassed. For another, what she was noticing was true.

Aunt Sylvia's a lot younger than Mrs. Weiss—she's twenty-eight or something. But she looks like Mrs. Weiss. She could be a model if she wanted to, but she wouldn't. She's studying for her Ph.D. in history at Columbia University.

"How are your mom and dad?" she asked Rachel. "How're they doing?"

"O.K., I guess," Rachel said. "It's sort of hard to tell."

"It's so *tough* for them right now," Aunt Sylvia said, "and for you. So many changes all at once. I wish I could do something, but what *can* I do, except wish you'll all be happy."

I never thought before about all the people who could feel sad when two people get divorced. Not only their children, but their friends and their family. I wondered if Rachel's mother and father had told their own parents yet, and whether their parents would *scold* them about it. It was good that Rachel had a relative as understanding as Aunt Sylvia.

"It's so good that you two have each other," she said just then, as though she and I had ESP.

Rachel took her camera out and started fooling with

it. "It's different, though, when your best friend lives in another place."

"Sure it is," Aunt Sylvia said. "But after all, you won't be at opposite ends of the earth. There are cars and buses—and phones." She turned to me. "Know where my best friend lives? Bloomington, Indiana. Indiana! I wouldn't want to show you my phone bills with the long-distance calls to Bloomington on them! Kathy and I have a pact—twice a month we splurge on a call and talk as long as we feel like it. I haven't seen her for six months, but I'm much closer to her than to people I see every day."

"I bet Mom will let me call Annie a lot," Rachel said.

"Of course she will," said Aunt Sylvia. "Your mom wants to do everything she can to make this easier for you."

"Besides," I said, "I'll visit a lot." I really would like to. It would be neat to learn my way around New York. Rachel and I could explore together. We could go to more museums and to plays and concerts. "Maybe we could even sell an article, like to *New York Magazine*, about things for kids to do in the city," I said.

"Neat." Rachel put her camera up to her face, focused on my dirty feet, and snapped.

"Rach! They're filthy!"

Aunt Sylvia stood up. "You kids better get your showers. Bruce and Erica will be here at five."

I'd almost forgotten! I wished we didn't have to see

them. I would much rather have stayed with Aunt Sylvia. "You go first," I told Rachel. I leaned back against the couch and watched Aunt Sylvia move some books from one side of the floor to the other.

"It's lucky I live alone," she said ruefully. "There wouldn't be room for another human being with all these books."

"Do you think you'll ever get married?" I asked her suddenly. Then I was embarrassed that I had. But she didn't act offended.

"I've thought about it," she said. "I don't know. Back when Denny married Clay, nobody even considered whether to or not. It was just what you *did*. Nowadays it's tougher because you know about the choices. You know getting married's not the only way to be happy. I *like* living alone." She wedged a book onto the shelf. "Still. I think it would be fabulous to find someone that you'd like to marry and grow older with, and share it all."

It seemed strange that someone as old as Aunt Sylvia would talk about growing up. In a way I'm not sure I like the idea that you always keep on doing it. It seems sort of tiring. And then, people don't automatically do it right.

"Sometimes getting married doesn't work out right," I said, thinking of the Weisses. "It's too bad you can't predict it before you waste time falling in love and having kids and all that—"

"It's not a waste," Aunt Sylvia interrupted. "It's *not*,

Annie. Denny and Clay's marriage wasn't a waste! They had a lot of good years and a lot of love. And they had Rachel. It's sad that they're breaking up. It's hard on all of them. But it's not a waste."

I thought of all the good times I'd had with the Weisses. In spite of everything, they did get a lot of love out of it. "It's a risk, though," I said.

"Sure. *Life's* pretty risky, when you get down to it."

I suddenly remembered Nora. "Nora died," I said.

"Oh, Annie!" Aunt Sylvia came over and hugged me. "Oh, I'm so sorry!" She held me quietly for a minute. "I only saw her a couple of times when I was out, but I thought she was one of the most beautiful dogs I'd ever seen. She looked like a deer when she bounced through the snow after you."

"I miss her a lot," I said.

"Oh, you must."

"What's the matter?" Rachel came in wearing a towel, with her hair dripping over her face. She blinked. She always looks naked without her glasses.

"I told her about Nora," I said.

"Oh," said Rachel. "I forgot you didn't know, Syl."

"No. It's sad." For a minute no one said anything. Then Aunt Sylvia gave me a little shove. "You'd better get your shower, Annie."

The cool water felt wonderful. I let it splash over me, thinking about the day. It seemed like a very long time since Rachel and I had started out in Madison. So many things had happened—the museum and the subways and that crazy fight and the dresses. Talking with Aunt Sylvia. Somehow, I felt very calm and peaceful with her. I wished we could just hang around at her place, and not have to meet Bruce and Erica. All the time I was dressing I got more and more nervous about it. I just knew they'd put me down or ignore me or talk with Rachel about things I didn't understand. I'm so stupid. I always think the worst like that. The one thing that never occurred to me was that they would be *nice*. But they were.

They were both tall and good-looking. Erica's blond hair was beautiful. They were wearing jeans and T-shirts, and the minute I saw them I felt overdressed. But then Erica started complimenting us on the dresses and asking where we got them, and Bruce said he recognized me from Rachel's description, and Aunt Sylvia sort of pushed us out the door, saying she wished *she* was going to a restaurant instead of eating deli food at home while she studied, and before I had time to feel uncomfortable we were out on the street.

We began to walk four across, but some kids with transistor radios shoved between us. Somehow Rachel and Erica got in front, and I was walking alone with Bruce. I didn't know what to talk about, but the sidewalk was full of people and music was blaring out of a record store so we didn't really have to say anything. It was sort of pleasant walking along like that.

Then all of a sudden Bruce grabbed my arm and

pulled me toward a store window. "You have to see these," he said. Three black and white puppies were rolling around on the sawdust in the window. They were small and pudgy with little bare pink stomachs. They were so cute I wanted to cry.

"That black-eared one is best," Bruce said. "He has the most spirit."

"Yeah." I was afraid to say anything more.

"Do you have a dog?" he asked, just as I knew he would.

"No." I watched the black-eared puppy slide off another one's back.

"*I'd* have one, if I lived in the country. That's the first thing I'd do, is get a dog."

It was getting worse and worse. I had to tell him. "I had a dog," I said. "Her name was Nora. She was really beautiful." I stopped a minute to make sure I wouldn't cry. "She died," I said. "About two weeks ago."

"Hey, I'm sorry!" Bruce turned away from the window abruptly, looking embarrassed.

"It's O.K.," I said. "It was neat to see the puppies. They're awfully cute." I wondered if they'd grow up to be as big as Nora. They wouldn't be as beautiful as Nora. No dog could be. They'd be nice in a different way.

We walked along for a while without saying anything. A woman in a sari walked by, holding a little Indian boy in a Ronald McDonald shirt by the hand.

"Anyway," I said suddenly, surprising myself as the words came out, "some day I'll probably get another dog." I paused. "Not for a long time, though. But some time." It was strange how happy I felt saying it. I guess I'd been wanting to say it all along, but I hadn't been ready until then.

All of a sudden the evening felt wonderful. Bruce and I ran to the corner to catch up to Rachel and Erica, and then we all ran down the street to the Greek restaurant they had picked out and crowded in the door, laughing. Erica led us through the front room and past the kitchen to a little outdoor garden, where strings of colored lights were hanging above tables with checked cloths on them. It was so neat! We found a table and sat down and the waiter gave us all menus. I couldn't understand a word on mine.

"It's all Greek to me," I said, and everyone laughed. Rachel looked at me in a pleased way, and I smiled back at her. There was a candle burning on our table, and Greek music was playing somewhere. I sat back in my chair with my dress falling around my ankles while they talked about Barclay. It sounded like a neat school, really. It was good Rachel would already have friends when she went there. They'd probably get to be my friends, too. I could see that her moving wasn't going to be the end of the world. It was the beginning of a lot of new stuff, and I'd be part of some of it.

But I still dreaded her actual move.

12

Rachel's moving day was the most beautiful day of June. I sat on the porch steps waiting for her to come over, feeling the hot sun on my legs and breathing in the mock-orange smell that reminded me of all our other summers. This summer would be so different. No Nora to run after us, panting, when we took off on our bikes. And no Rachel to go off with. There would be lots of things to do—I had signed up for ceramics classes in the summer program with Sue and Janie, and Angela was having a sleep-over party, and Debbie was probably going to have a swimming party with boys if her mother said yes. It would be fun, but it would all be different. I would miss Rachel so much.

"Hi, Annie!" Peter James had come up the driveway without my even noticing. He was wearing a T-shirt and cutoffs. "Waiting for something?"

"For Rachel. She's moving to the city today." Saying it made it seem more real.

"I didn't know she was going so soon." Peter came up the steps. He already had a tan. I think boys who are blond look especially good with tans. "Maybe some day this summer you and Ken and I could bike out to Blue Lake," he said. "If you wanted to."

I was surprised. He must have noticed I was getting older. "Sure, neat," I said, too pleased to try to act cool.

Kenny came down to let Peter in, and I leaned back against the steps. It was strange to think about doing things without Rachel. And to know she'd be doing stuff in the city without me. I wondered how long it would take before I'd stop feeling either guilty or jealous. Maybe not that long, once she actually moved. Maybe waiting for it to happen was the worst part.

A car honked and came up the driveway. It was *starting* to happen! Suddenly I felt scared. I didn't want it to.

"Close your eyes!" Rachel shouted, climbing out of the car.

I closed them. She sounded so natural I felt better. I heard the other car door open and Mr. Weiss say, "Easy, easy." Rachel said, "I've got it," and Mr. Weiss said, "Don't let it drop. Hold your side up a little bit." I couldn't figure out what was going on.

"Don't open your eyes till we tell you," Rachel warned, coming closer. They came slowly up the steps and set something down on the porch. "Now!" Rachel said.

I opened my eyes. The doll house! With all the furniture and everything. "Oh, Rach!" I jumped up and hugged her. *"Thanks!"* Then I realized. "But you'll miss it so much!"

Rachel's face clouded for a second. "There wouldn't be room in the apartment," she said. Her mother had found a pretty good one near Aunt Sylvia's, but it was small. "It's better for you to have it here."

"This way," Mr. Weiss said, "the house will have a good home!" I could tell he was trying hard to be cheery. He held out his arms to me. "Well, Annie—"

I hugged him. He felt so nice and solid. I would miss him. "I'll miss you," I said.

"Thanks." He kissed the top of my head. "Well, girls." He tried to smile. "Mom's going to pick you up, Rachel. In about an hour."

An hour! We watched him get into the car and drive away.

"What do you want to do?" I asked. There wasn't time to do anything.

"I don't know. There's no *time,*" Rachel said.

We stood there looking at the doll house. The little plants in the attic window were bright in the sun. I could see the fourposter bed behind them. "You know what I always wanted to do?" I said. "Make a patchwork quilt for the fourposter."

"That would take days!"

"Yeah, but we could start on it now, and then each of us do more and put it together the next time."

"Yeah, sure we could," Rachel said fairly enthusiastically.

So I got Mom's scrap basket and scissors and we sat down with our backs against the porch railings and pulled out pieces of cloth and started to cut them up. There were some nice scraps, including a piece of flowery material big enough for a lot of squares. I was glad I'd thought of a quilt. It was a good long project.

"I'll take good care of the doll house, Rach," I said, cutting into the cloth. "You won't have to worry about it. I'll keep it clean and water the plants and all—"

Rachel looked up. "Listen, Annie," she said carefully. "I don't want you to think I expect you to keep it in your room forever or anything."

"I *will*, though!" Even as I said it I wasn't positive. It's hard to predict how you'll feel. Before, I used to think you could.

"You know how, in books, the kids put their doll houses away in the attic when they grow up?" Rachel asked. "Maybe you could do that. It would be nice to always know it was there, even when we're old."

"Oh, yes! We could keep it there forever! And then our kids could go up to the attic and find it. If we *had* any." It was strange to imagine us with kids.

"It's strange to imagine us with kids," Rachel said.

"Yeah." I wondered if our ESP would work when

Rachel moved. It probably would. She wasn't going *that* far. "I don't see why people want to try to predict the future," I said. "Just getting used to the present is complicated enough."

"I know it," said Rachel.

"Hey, where'd you get *that*?" Kenny came out with Peter and looked down at the doll house. "Isn't that Rachel's?"

"She gave it to me, just now." I hoped he'd realize what an important present it was, and not make some mean remark.

"Hey, that was nice of you, Rachel," he said, as though he understood. He grabbed Rachel's hand and sort of shook it. "Well. In case I don't see you," he said quite formally, "good luck with everything." He let her hand go. "We'll miss you."

Rachel smiled up at him. "Thanks, Kenny."

Then Peter tapped her shoulder and said, "So long, Rachel," and they went down the steps and off somewhere.

The good-byes had made me nervous. I suddenly remembered. "Rach! I forgot your present!"

"I didn't know there *was* one."

I poked her. "That's the point, dope—it's a surprise!" I ran inside for the book. That morning, before I wrapped it, I had written a poem inside:

> You may go away
> But you leave behind

105

Happy memories
Like pictures in my mind.

I held the package in my hand for a minute. I suddenly felt shy. Then I gave it to Rachel.

"It's a beautiful package," she said shyly. Neither of us had any practice with good-bye gifts before.

"Open it!"

Rachel untied the ribbon and pulled the paper off. The book was upside down. I can't ever wrap a book so the title comes out on top.

Rachel turned it over. Then she gasped. "Oh, *Annie!* Oh, wow, that's so neat! *Thanks!*" She opened the cover and read my poem. "Oh, it's beautiful! You're such a good writer!" She had started to cry. "Thank you! I'll treasure it for my whole life." She took off her glasses and wiped her eyes on her sleeve. Then she turned the pages, blinking.

"You wouldn't believe how hard it was not to tell you!" I said.

"I'm glad you didn't, Annie. It's such a wonderful surprise."

There was a honk. We both jumped. Mrs. Weiss was in the driveway.

She got out of the car and came toward us.

"Mom, look what Annie gave me!" Rachel held out the book.

Mrs. Weiss took it. "Oh, Annie—what a beautiful gift!" She opened the book and read my poem and burst into tears. "Oh, dear," she said, fumbling for a tissue. "I didn't mean to do that! I told myself before I came, 'Now, don't go *crying* at the last minute, when the girls have done so well.' " She wiped her eyes.

Mom came out on the porch, with two pots of garden mint. "How are you, Denny?"

"I'm O.K." Mrs. Weiss blew her nose and tried to smile. "Annie's poem just did me in for a minute."

"I hope you'll have room for this," Mom said, giving her the mint. "I thought you'd like something green on your windowsills, you and Clayton."

That was thoughtful of Mom. But the idea of *two* pots—one for Rachel and her mother and the other for her father's separate home—was so sad. I tightened up, not wanting to cry.

"Thanks." Mrs. Weiss patted Mom's arm. Then she hugged me. Mom hugged Rachel. I could tell it was coming.

"Rachel." Mrs. Weiss started down the steps. "We really have to go."

I picked up the squares we'd cut out and handed Rachel half of them, wordlessly. She and I stared at each other.

"So long, Rach," I said.

We grabbed each other and hung on. Then Rachel pulled away, ran to the car, and came back with a brown envelope. She handed it to me. "Here. I didn't know when to give it to you."

I stood there holding the envelope while she got in

the car. I could see her glasses through the windshield. The car backed slowly away.

"Good-bye!" I called after it. "Good-bye, Rach!"

Mom kissed me quickly and went inside. She knows when you need to be alone. I sat down on the steps and opened the envelope and pulled out a photograph.

It was Nora! She looked so *real*. She was curled up in the sunlight asleep, with her head over her paw. It must have been that day when we tried to teach her tricks.

"Oh, Nora," I said. "Oh, Nora, you were so beautiful!" I wished so much that she could come alive, just even for a minute, and curl up in my lap and comfort me with her soft weight.

The leaves on the bush behind Nora were just little buds in the picture. I tried to remember how warm it had seemed to us then, and how happy we were that spring had started to come. That was such a long time ago! Rachel and I were so different then, before everything happened. We were like children. I remembered how I had wished we would never grow up and that things would never change. In the back of my mind I must have known they would.

I let myself sit there and cry for a while, in memory of the way we had been. Then I got up and went inside.

BETTY MILES is well known for her truthful and engaging novels, including *The Real Me, Just the Beginning, All It Takes Is Practice* and *Looking On,* as well as for her many books for younger readers.

A graduate of Antioch College, Betty Miles has taught children's literature at Bank Street College and has also been on the staff of the Bank Street publications division. She lives with her husband in Rockland County, New York. They have three grown children.